ANNIE'S RECIPE

Also by Lisa Jones Baker

THE HOPE CHEST OF DREAMS SERIES

Rebecca's Bouquet

ANTHOLOGIES

The Amish Christmas Kitchen
(with Kelly Long
and Jennifer Beckstrand)

The Amish Christmas Candle
(with Kelly Long
and Jennifer Beckstrand)

Published by Kensington Publishing Corporation

ANNIE'S RECIPE

Lisa Jones Baker

ZEBRA BOOKS
KENSINGTON PUBLISHING CORP.
http://www.kensingtonbooks.com

ZEBRA BOOKS are published by

Kensington Publishing Corp.
119 West 40th Street
New York, NY 10018

All Kensington titles, imprints, and distributed lines are available at special quantity discounts for bulk purchases for sales promotion, premiums, fund-raising, educational, or institutional use.

Special book excerpts or customized printings can also be created to fit specific needs. For details, write or phone the office of the Kensington Sales Manager: Attn.: Sales Department. Kensington Publishing Corp., 119 West 40th Street, New York, NY 10018. Phone: 1-800-221-2647.

First Printing: March 2017
ISBN-13: 978-1-4201-4154-2
ISBN-10: 1-4201-4154-6

eISBN-13: 978-1-4201-4155-9
eISBN-10: 1-4201-4155-4

10 9 8 7 6 5 4 3 2

Printed in the United States of America

To John and Marcia Baker, my dearest friends

Acknowledgments

I'm beholden to my Lord and Savior for blessing me with publication after twenty-four years of prayers to see my stories in print. My kind, loving mother, Marcia, former librarian and reading specialist, deserves tremendous credit for attentively listening to me read my novels out loud for over two decades. To Beth Zehr, sister extraordinaire: Thanks for taking on my numerous laptop and formatting challenges. Also, much appreciation to Doug Zehr, Gary Kerr, Brooke and Brittany for their important contributions. A special thank you to Bloomington Geek Squad expert Elizabeth Ray. Tons of gratitude to Amber Kauffman, former executive director, Illinois Amish Interpretive Center, for answering and clarifying numerous inquisitions. To the friendly, wonderful folks in the Arthur/Tuscola, Illinois, area who have graciously entertained my questions, shared special stories, and even allowed me inside their homes. Of course I can't forget the Cheese Festival individuals and the Arthur Welcome Center. Many thanks to Steve Followell, Fire Chief at Weldon Community Fire Protection District.

I'd like to extend special appreciation to writer Lisa Norato, true friend, critique partner, and writing confidante, and to hundreds of other authors, published and unpublished, who have evaluated my material through contests and in private. Immense gratitude to Joan Wester Anderson for endorsing my debut novel, *Rebecca's Bouquet*, and for invaluable input.

I'm indebted to my fabulous Amish go-to girl who prefers to remain anonymous while loyally reviewing my rough drafts, front to back. Your unique way of life has my full respect, appreciation, and admiration.

Last, but certainly not least, a heartfelt thank you to my tenacious agent, Tamela Hancock Murray, who believed in me from the get-go; Kensington Books; and to my incredible editor, Selena James.

Prologue

Annie Mast tossed a rock into Pebble Creek and giggled. She clapped her hands as the small stone hit the water. Beside her, Levi Miller nodded his approval. Their contest was always who could make the bigger splash. Of course Levi usually won. But she guessed when her efforts trumped his, it was because he allowed it. After all, at eight years of age, it wasn't easy competing with a twelve-year-old boy. Especially a boy much taller and stronger than she was.

Levi joined in the applause. "If you keep throwing like that, I'll have to practice."

Annie grinned. Automatically, they stepped side by side up the incline leading to their sitting spot. Hills were unusual in predominantly flat Illinois, but she was sure God had planned this particular elevation especially for her and Levi.

Without talking, she claimed her stone at the same time he declared his. Not wasting a moment,

Annie reached into the wicker basket between them for a sponge cake. Levi accepted the napkin-covered, sweet-smelling dessert with an appreciative grin. As he did so, she automatically took in the curve of his high cheekbones and determined jaw. Brightness lightened his autumn-brown hair a shade. As always, he waited to bite into the treat until she held hers between her fingers. Together, they ate while the late August sun caressed them. In her long Amish dress and apron, Annie quickly forgot the unusually hot temperature when Levi pointed to Old Sam Beachy's barn.

"You want to know a secret?"

She lifted an inquisitive brow while anxiously awaiting the response.

"One day you'll be as good a cook as Esther."

Annie's heart smiled. Everyone knew Sam's wife made the best dishes around.

Excitement edged Annie's voice. "You really think so?"

He took another bite before offering a quick, definitive nod and lowered his pitch to a whisper. She wondered why. There wasn't anyone within hearing distance.

"There's no doubt in my mind."

Annie's heart jumped with happiness. Even more than matching Esther's baking skills, what really mattered was that she and her best friend were together. And as long as she was with Levi, how could life get better?

Chapter One

If not for the strong arm that reached out to break her fall, Annie Mast would have ended up on the ground. As she balanced herself, two kids playing tag uttered a quick apology. Shaking her head at their boisterous play, Annie turned to thank her rescuer and locked gazes with a hazel-eyed man and froze. He was English, and there weren't many Englishers at the Amish wedding. But that wasn't what made the words catch in her throat.

"Annie?"

She gasped. "Levi?" Levi Miller? Could it be? In her mind she saw the Amish boy, her one and only best childhood friend. Her confidant until that terrible day.

He gently released his hold on her. But they continued to regard each other, taking in how more than ten years had changed their appearances. Even though he'd taken his hand from her arm, his warmth still penetrated her skin and traveled up to her shoulder.

A man's touch wasn't proper, but he'd rescued her. All the same, the result was reassuring, and she was sure she would never forget the comforting sensation. For an awkward moment they regarded each other with curiosity. The sudden lack of words took her by surprise, but then, they hadn't crossed paths for nearly a decade.

Still, it didn't matter. Directly in front of her stood the dear boy she'd trusted years ago, and even though circumstances had changed, their strong bond hadn't.

"I've missed you, Annie."

Annie swallowed an emotional knot as she took in the words that mimicked her own thoughts. Suddenly recalling why they were both there, Annie tried to put a damper on her excitement at seeing Levi and changed the subject to the first thing she could think of. "It's a nice day, isn't it?"

Before he could respond, she threw her hands in the air and raised the pitch of her voice to be heard over the crowd. "I've never seen your cousin Jeremiah look so happy. Katie's good for him."

Levi offered a nod of agreement. "It's wonderful seeing them together. And you're right about the weather. But . . ."

He took in a deep breath before donning a full-blown grin. "I forgot how long Amish weddings are! It's nice to finally stand." He stretched a pair of strong-looking arms in front of him and interlaced his fingers. The gesture was followed by a sigh of relief.

He laughed and she joined him. The sun brightened a notch, and she blinked in reaction. A mélange of happy voices floated around her, morphing into one solid sound. The tent was packed.

A long queue of black buggies and brown-haired horses loomed nearby, behind a couple of large refrigeration vehicles. The enticing aroma of homemade dishes filled her nostrils, reminding her that she hadn't eaten for hours.

But she barely paid attention to anything other than Levi's full-grown, head-to-toe appearance. His boyish looks had matured. Of course she shouldn't be shocked.

Parted at the side, autumn-brown hair that met the tops of his ears had taken on a slightly darker shade, almost matching the hue of his skin. The confident curve of his lips echoed high, proud cheekbones. With a swift motion, he shoved some rebellious strands of hair off his forehead.

She covered her mouth with her fingers as a giggle edged with sudden nervousness escaped her mouth. "You're so . . . tall!"

The sunlight landed on his eyes, and they sparkled. "Mom's the same ol' good cook she always was. But you, Annie . . ."

His expression filled with approval. "You've changed a little. You've still got that contagious laugh." He gave a slight nod. "You've thinned up. And you're taller." He winked and lowered the pitch of his voice. "But I see that mischievous sparkle in your eyes I remember all too well. I can't wait to hear what you've been up to."

At the same time, they stepped aside to allow a group of men who transported a wooden bench to pass.

Warmth from a nearby gas heater floated up Annie's back. In reaction, she breathed in delight. The month of October had brought a sudden drop in temperature.

But her attention lingered on Levi and their conversation. Annie was fully aware that she had gradually dropped weight over the years and supposed that was partly due to her growth spurt. She wasn't thin by any means but never worried about it.

"Remember when we used to plan a trip together to Six Flags during *Rumspringa*?"

She nodded and lowered her voice to a more confidential, eager tone. "Surely we can talk?"

Annie was determined not to lose him again without having caught up. But she was fully aware that all eyes would be on her spending time with someone "English." So be it. The Amish weren't by any means exclusive in conversations; it was just that they tried to avoid close relationships with outsiders to keep away from temptations they wouldn't otherwise be exposed to. However, nothing could stop her from spending as much time as she could with Levi.

"How long will you be here?"

"A few days. Dad needs me at work."

Her heart sank. But what had she expected? He no longer lived in Arthur, Illinois. And because his father had been shunned, she guessed she was fortunate to see him this once.

A short silence ensued. "The rest of the day's pretty much spoken for." He paused and his eyes widened with reassurance. "You know I wouldn't leave town without talking to my Annie. You free tomorrow?"

She gave an eager nod, suddenly remembering she was supposed to be a food server in the tent.

"How about we meet at Pebble Creek?"

Later that day, Levi scooted up the front seat of his uncle's buggy to allow Cousin Jake into the back. Levi helped hoist the five-year-old up into the two metal foot holders until his narrow hips landed on the bench. The youngster smiled at him with large brown, hopeful eyes.

At the reins, Uncle Marlin leaned forward, extending his arms in front of him. At the moment, the most peaceful, familiar sensation swept through Levi's body. The rush of unexpected happiness swept down his back and landed in his feet. He recalled how his uncle used buggy time to reflect on the day.

"Nice wedding."

Levi agreed and moved slightly as the horse pulled forward. Bullet threw his head up, gave it a quick shake, and whinnied. Hooves against blacktop was the only noise besides an occasional sniffle from Jake. The poor kid had a bad case of allergies.

The uneven clop-clopping resonated through the cool fall air. While the queue of horses took off down the country road, an unexpected warmth tugged at Levi's heart.

Above, the sun set in the west. As the round, orange light dimmed, a kaleidoscope of colors loomed miraculously around it, as if a painter had spilled several different shades onto a canvas.

From his peripheral vision, he glimpsed Jake glancing out of the small side window. Without warning, Annie's happy face popped into Levi's mind. A sigh of complete satisfaction escaped him. When they had spoken, their long-lost friendship had flooded his entire body like a much-needed rain. He gave a slow, uncertain shake of his head. Where had the past ten years gone?

As their buggy traversed the bumpy road, details about Annie floated through his mind until he could see her perfectly clearly.

He'd noted everything, from the enthusiastic sparkle in her eyes that was a unique combination of mischievousness and fun to the energetic tone he'd never been able to say no to. He'd always loved the light, eager pitch that edged her voice and her full, generous smile. Even today, the energy in her eyes had made him think of embarking on a new adventure with her.

He pressed his lips together with unexpected interest while considering her soft blond hair parted in the middle. The thick mass pulled tightly under a covering had turned to a light honey color. The shade made her flawless skin take on a creamier appearance.

He tapped his foot nervously as her breathtaking features carefully etched their striking details into his mind. What fascinated him most were her clear aquamarine eyes. To his astonishment, the piercing blue-green reminded him of beautiful pictures of the Pacific Ocean he'd glimpsed in the AAA travel agency window. She'd always had them of course. But for some reason he had taken special notice today.

He pushed out a lazy breath and rested a firm hand on his hip. If he gazed into the predominantly blue depths long enough, surely he would drown with contentment.

The small brown freckle under her right eye that he'd teased her about as a kid had developed into something of a beauty mark. It belonged there. To his dismay, his pulse picked up speed. He wanted more time with her. She was of *Rumspringa* age, so she could do non-Amish things. But that would only be for a couple of years, not forever.

Behind them, Aunt Abigail followed in a separate buggy with Aidan and Elijah. As Levi glanced back at Jake, the kid responded with a big grin. To Levi's surprise, an unexpected appreciation for the ambience in the buggy, often referred to as the fiberglass box, welled in his chest. He sat back as the horses stepped it up.

Automatically, Levi looked down. There wasn't a trace of dirt on the beautiful navy velvet cushion that softened the hard bench. He remembered when his mother had used a lint brush to clean their buggy. On the sides were two small viewing windows and one in the back. A blue homemade quilt was rolled up and slightly draped over the backseat. He'd forgotten what it was like being in a means of transportation with no seat belts or radio. Levi missed the music. He was used to driving his dad's truck and had traversed country roads long before he'd gotten his license a few years before.

As they traveled, Levi glanced back to smile at little Jake. The response was a large toothless grin and eyes wide with excitement. Levi knew the child was dying to spend time with him.

Levi had nearly decided not to come today. Even though there had been no mention of the shunning, everyone knew it had happened. He had never discussed it with anyone. He and Annie had shared everything when they were young. And despite their unbreakable bond, she was still Amish.

I've got to stop thinking about her.

The sound of wind knocking long evergreen branches against the siding made Annie glance at her bedroom window. She thought back over the day and pushed out a satisfied sigh. A yawn escaped her, and she automatically pressed her palm over her lips.

She'd witnessed wonderful blessings: a wedding, family and friends who celebrated Katie and Jeremiah's new beginning together, Levi . . .

The very thought of him caused her pulse to pick up to a happy speed. She didn't want to forget him.

With one swift motion, she jumped up from her sitting position on her oak-framed bed and proceeded to the hope chest Old Sam had made just for her. With great concentration, she traced her finger over the design of a sponge cake recipe on the oak wood lid and smiled.

She loved the widower and looked after him with two friends, Rebecca and Rachel. She had been close to his wife. Esther had made sponge cakes for practically everyone around. After her death, Annie had adopted a motherly attitude toward the old man, who treated her like a granddaughter.

Annie's heart warmed as she considered the unique situation. Rebecca picked him fresh wildflowers in the spring and summer. Annie kept him well-fed with delicious sponge cakes. And Rachel, the youngest, listened for hours while he recounted horse-and-buggy stories.

She was fully aware how unusual it was for an Amish man to have such a close connection with three young girls. Under different circumstances, it might not have been acceptable. Yet the relationships were a blessing. Sam was an exception. Everyone loved him and wanted to befriend the hope chest maker, and fortunately, in this case, the community didn't object to his closeness with them.

Annie wondered what Sam would say if he knew what she was feeling for Levi. She stopped and tapped her bare foot against the shiny hardwood floor. What were her sentiments exactly? And why couldn't she rid Levi from her mind?

Because he's in town. And because I can't wait to hear what he's been up to the past decade.

Automatically, she opened the lid and reached inside for her journal and pen. A sigh of immediate relief escaped her. Blank lined pages were her way to figure things out. For some reason, when she penned her thoughts, logical answers came to her. And right now she needed to think through her reunion with her childhood friend and the many emotions that sparked.

She got comfortable on the floor and rested against the fragrant pine bedframe. Touching the soft cotton quilt Mamma had made with so much love and patience, she crossed her legs and began to write, starting with the date.

Today was wonderful. Jeremiah and Katie were married.

She paused to consider the chaos and smiled a little.

It sounds simple. But there were so many details that went into the day. Tons of work. I guess I could start with the husband and wife. Katie looked beautiful in her homemade sky-blue dress and shiny black high-top shoes.

And Jeremiah was handsome in his black vest and bow tie. To my surprise, neither appeared nervous. On the contrary, the expressions on their faces were of pure joy and excitement. In fact, Katie's cheeks glowed. As I watched them, I couldn't help but wonder what I would feel like in her place. With my husband-to-be.

An uncertain sigh escaped her throat as she stretched her bare toes. She hesitated before continuing.

I wish I could imagine myself in her shoes.

Annie squeezed her eyes closed and struggled to picture herself as a bride. Finally, she rolled her eyes in frustration and giggled in defeat.

Even my keen imagination won't allow me to go there.

She tapped the tip of her pen nervously against the paper before continuing.

Maybe it's because I'm afraid. Perhaps the reason is because it's impossible for me to envision the face of the man next to me.

Suddenly, an uncomfortable ache in the pit of her stomach prompted her to change her thoughts. And that was easy; the day had encompassed a vast array of events.

The food was wonderful. That's where we Amish women excel. As I took in all the casseroles, I was sure I would need an extra plate. Of course I wasn't surprised at the number of edibles. Amish weddings are certainly known for their abundance of homemade dishes. But today must have been the largest selection I've ever seen. And I've attended a lot of weddings. I enjoyed everything from baked chicken and mashed potatoes and gravy to corn casserole and yummy dumplings. The dumplings were the best. Of course I'm not surprised. Rebecca Conrad's mamma made them. She even sells them. I also indulged in an extra piece of pecan pie.

Annie shifted her hips to a more comfortable position and licked her lips.

Mamma doesn't like pecans, so I have to take advantage of the delicious desserts when the opportunity presents itself. Mamma's a great cook; I'm not complaining. But no one in the world is 100 percent perfect.

The day was bright and sunny. Kids played tag outside of the tent. The queue of buggies lined up must have been a mile long. And two refrigeration trucks were parked alongside them.

Before the wedding, word had it that there might not be enough plates and silverware. Even with the family members pitching in. That Katie's mamma used every resource she had to round up more dishes and utensils. She must have come through because no one went without.

Even though so many blessings were right in front of my eyes, there was one that stood out.

Her heart skipped a beat as she paused.

Something wonderful and unexpected happened. Levi Miller came to the wedding. Meeting up with him was the best gift anyone could have given me.

She rested her hands on her lap and looked ahead, remembering the warmth and tenderness in his eyes as their gazes had locked. Recalling vividly the genuine emotion in his voice when he'd told her he'd missed her. She smiled a little.

I can't believe a decade has passed since he lived here. I recall with great joy our strong friendship and the fun we shared. At our young age, people always commented on how unusual our deep bond was. Most of the other girls thought the boys were silly. And the boys considered the girls ridiculous. But my friendship with Levi was different. And rare.

She frowned.

I respect my faith with all my heart but wish our differences didn't build a wall between Levi and me. But I didn't decide on the Ordnung. *And I certainly can't change the rules.*

She stretched her legs and lowered her head against the covering. As soon as she pushed out a deep sigh, her thoughts returned to Levi.

I realize how much I've missed him. If only we could forget what happened to his father and pick up where we left off. Oh, why do we have to be on different teams?

She shrugged her shoulders to rid the knot making its way down her arm. A team. Was that what faith was? Was each religion a different club? Didn't God want His followers to be on the same one? And did it matter if they weren't? As long as they all believed?

She giggled as an analogy came to mind and grinned as she wrote.

Each church is like a delicious two-layered chocolate cake. Each cook puts the ingredients together differently. Yet the results look and taste pretty much the same.

She considered differences in faith and raised an inquisitive brow. Early on, her sister and cousins had grown up with their to-be spouses. Their marriage partners had been no surprise.

When I was young, Levi and I shared our hopes and dreams with each other. Talked about what we wanted to do when we grew up. Planned a trip to Six Flags once we were in Rumspringa. *One evening, when we were walking home from the singing, Levi even mentioned getting married when we got older. While other kids our age usually weren't close to members of the opposite sex, the bond between Levi and me grew stronger whenever we spent time together. And it all started with Pebble Creek.*

Thinking of the place prompted a sigh of contentment.

The first time we met at the beautiful place was accidental. It was that day when we each confessed our dream to live there. It's funny that it connected us in a way I never dreamed was possible. After that, we met there whenever we could.

We were kids. The world was simple. I always thought of him as my protector. With Levi, I never feared anything. Our friendship was all I needed to be happy. Things have changed.

The excited speed of her pulse slowed as her glass half-full attitude kicked in. She made a silent vow to stay positive. She knew the world didn't always present perfect situations.

She considered Levi's broad shoulders and long legs. Black polished shoes. Confident walk. The way he lifted his chin.

The way he carries himself shouts to the world that he's still Levi Miller and that he can handle anything that comes his way. No problem was ever too large for him.

In all my eighteen years, I've yearned to talk to him as I used to. I've dreamed of taking long walks together. I can't wait for the chance. Even though Levi has come back to Arthur, I feel as if I'm the one who has come home.

It was hard to believe it was the first week of October. Levi changed into sweats after saying good night to Aunt Abigail, Uncle Marlin, and his younger cousins. He looked around the small bedroom and sighed with satisfaction. The wedding was over. Relief swept through his chest as he considered the long eventful day he had nearly passed on. He was glad he hadn't.

The simple invitation hadn't really surprised him. After all, he was family. But when Levi had pondered whether to come, to his astonishment, it had been his dad who had convinced him to do it. "I think it would be good for you, son. Who knows? This might bring you closure."

Levi's parents had also received invitations; they'd even discussed whether to attend. But in the end they hadn't been at ease returning, sitting at a different table from family. It wasn't uncommon for shunned people to pass.

Levi frowned. He wished for family unity, but that ship had sailed. Because the very people he'd been raised to love and respect had shunned his father.

He supposed there were worse things. Besides, a huge goal had been accomplished today: closure. Wasn't that really the reason he'd come? Levi recalled his agonizing drive from Morton to Arthur. He closed his eyes for a moment and wrung his fingers together in front of him. When he opened his lids, a sigh escaped him.

It had taken everything he had to return to the very place that had changed the course of his father's life. His entire family's life. To Levi's satisfaction, today had provided a most-needed relief. Finality.

He hadn't been sure of what to expect, but to his surprise, Levi had been treated as if nothing had happened. He had even been seated with his cousins, not at a table by himself. Of course he wasn't the one who'd been shunned. He couldn't be. He'd never joined the Amish church in the first place.

Still, he'd returned to his old world feeling like an outsider. And just because the shunning hadn't been mentioned didn't mean it hadn't occurred.

Levi hadn't neglected to notice that no one had inquired about his dad. Or his mom. *But what can I do about it? I have to accept what happened. To forgive and move on. Today I did that, didn't I?*

On a positive note, he had enjoyed meeting up with old friends. Some he had barely recognized. The past ten years had added height and weight and other surprising features to those with whom he'd shared his childhood. Even the young married men sported beards.

The recollection of his childhood friend, William Conrad, brought a smile to his face. He was the same as always yet different. Two years his senior, William had baled hay with him.

As they had spoken after dinner, William had told Levi about helping his ailing father, Daniel, who had also been shunned. Levi had been surprised to hear that William had even considered leaving the faith.

It had been his new wife, Rebecca, who had been the deciding factor in staying. The recent conversation stuck in Levi's mind. Though he and William hadn't talked about Levi's dad, Levi felt a strong bond with him because he had also experienced what shunning did.

If some day Levi chose to talk to anyone about the past, he was certain William would understand. But all through the day, despite friendly chatter, someone had pulled at his heart stronger than anyone else.

He cupped his hand with his chin and thought of Annie. He couldn't wait to catch up with her.

He knew how strict the Amish were about staying true to their beliefs. He wasn't a threat; still, people talked. And if they saw Annie with him alone, they would immediately worry about her deserting the only life she knew. Especially at such an impressionable age. If he wasn't careful, he could easily stir up a lot of gossip. Because of that realization, he would have to make his time with her brief.

Chapter Two

The following morning, the warm bright sun hovered between two large puffy clouds, reminding Annie of large, soft marshmallows.

Garments on Mamma's clothesline floated up and down as a gentle breeze pushed them. A chicken darted beneath a long-sleeved shirt and drifted toward Old Sam's barn. A redheaded rooster followed. Annie would never forget the time the mean old bird had chased her, pecking at her bare heels.

Annie thought of her beloved mentor. As she focused on his deep red barn in the distance, she pictured him with his faithful Irish setter, Buddy, at his side while he carefully dreamed up beautiful hope chests. But Sam's weren't ordinary designs; each was custom-made for the person who ordered it.

He was a talented artist. Something unique about his work made his art come alive. She had never seen anything like it.

Others had tried to do what Sam did, but no one,

so far, had succeeded. The chests were his specialty; he had inherited his trade from his father and granddad. In fact, Sam was well-known throughout the United States for his ability to craft unique art into beautiful walnut, oak, and cherry lids.

The chest he'd built for Annie was a precious reminder of their longtime friendship. And her love and respect for him had grown after the death of his wife. Annie had watched his weight drop and his smile lines disappear. Thank goodness he was okay now. And she looked up to Sam as if he were family.

When they talked, decades of age difference didn't matter. She did most of the chatting, but Sam spoke, too. He related childhood stories. He loved reminiscing about the horses that had driven his buggy over the years. About the coldest winter he'd ever known. About Esther's butterscotch pie. He'd lost her to pneumonia.

He'd put his most creative thoughts to work as he'd etched an image of the words of a simple sponge cake recipe into oak that had come from his family's lumber mill.

Since Esther had passed some years ago, Old Sam had produced more custom-made hope chests than anyone else in all the Amish communities combined. These works of art were passed down from generation to generation. Customers from all over ordered from him.

Annie walked through the open barn door as she always did. "Old Sam! It's Annie!"

She bounded inside at the same time Sam waved a welcoming hand, proudly displaying her platter of sponge cakes for him to admire.

Sam grinned and stepped toward her to retrieve the platter. As she handed it to him, Annie smiled. Sam plucked one, took a bite of the small cake, and nodded his satisfaction. She made sure Sam never went hungry. And, in return, as long as she had him, she could confide whatever was on her mind. Today she needed to talk to him about something. Some-*one*, actually: Levi Miller.

Later that day, Levi stood before the vacant fifteen-acre plot of land he had always loved. Pebble Creek was in between Annie's house and Old Sam's place.

To his chagrin, he couldn't rid Annie from his mind. Ten years ago circumstances beyond his control had torn them apart. But right now he was focused on moving forward. A gentle smile tugged at the corners of his lips as he pictured an imaginary self-built, two-story house.

He could almost see shiny hardwood floorboards with glossy polish and could nearly hear dry wood crackle in the fireplace. Beautiful hand-picked stones he had selected himself hovered artistically above it.

He stepped slowly to avoid the uneven earth and made his way to the creek that divided this lot and Annie's. When he stopped, his thoughts settled on his childhood best friend.

His heart skipped an excited beat. Her cheeks still turned red whenever she was embarrassed. He was sure she still spoke her mind. Absently, he wondered how she got along with other shy Amish girls.

That question prompted him to walk on. To his

side, water cascaded over a small fall and into the main creek that wound its way through the hill. Central Illinois was completely flat. Except for this lot. The unusual landscape made it even more special and rare.

The place was magical. But the most memorable part of the day wouldn't be the land. It would be the person he would meet. He looked off in the distance. Of course she'd always run late. His lips curved in amusement. Where was she?

Annie took quick steps from the barn to the house. Inside, she hung her wool coat on her hook. As she washed her hands, her mother was making buttermilk cheese.

Annie licked her lips. "I love your cheese more than anything in the world, Mamma. Everyone buys it these days. I'm so glad you still make it."

Annie stepped closer to look over her shoulder.

Her mother darted her a quick glance while she continued mixing cultured buttermilk into the pot. Mamma gave a slow swirl to the contents; from experience, Annie knew you had to be careful not to overstir. She noted new concern lines under her mother's eyes.

"Annie?"

Annie came back to reality. "Sorry, Mamma."

She faced a dubious expression. "You've got your mind on something." Her mother faced her. "It wouldn't be that Miller boy, would it?"

Annie pretended a sudden interest in cleaning

the sink, running her cotton towel over the stainless steel. "Why would you think that, Mamma?"

"Ever since yesterday, you've been acting like you're off in some other world." She lifted her palms to the sky. "You even forgot to close the door when you stepped outside. You *know* he lives different from us, Annie."

Her mother's statement had come out in a lowered, serious tone.

"I know, Mamma. But I still like him. Always did."

Suddenly, an uneasy feeling filled Annie's gut. She held the colander while Mamma carefully poured curds into it. Annie's favorite part of the process was hanging the curds to dry.

"Don't you think our community was a bit harsh on Levi's dad?"

"Honey, the *Ordnung* has been around for years. Those who choose not to follow it know the repercussions. Rules are rules."

Still holding the colander, which became heavier by the second, Annie focused on keeping it perfectly still. Her arms shook a little. "But wouldn't God want us to forgive?"

Her mother pushed out a sigh as the last drop of yellowish mixture came out of the stainless-steel cooker. Hot steam hit her face. Annie was glad to return the colander to the sink and step away from the intense heat.

She sat down on a beautiful dark walnut chair made by her father and looked up. Annie searched her mom's face and awaited a response. None came. But it didn't matter. Annie knew what her answer was.

* * *

With a combination of uncertainty and great excitement, Annie approached Pebble Creek. The crisp fall air smelled of burned leaves; neighbors had cleaned their yards. A light haze of smoke lingered before evaporating into the environment.

As she took in the vast area that led to Pebble Creek, she breathed in slowly and appreciatively and pressed her lips together in awe. The land was beautiful, and this particular parcel boasted the only hill in the predominantly flat area.

Annie looked around; she stepped carefully, occasionally lifting the bottom of her dress so as not to trip on sudden inclines in the ground. As her left foot succumbed to a hole, she quickly caught herself to avoid a fall. Regaining her balance, she carefully began to increase the speed of her pace, anxious to see Levi.

She considered the significance of their meeting, and automatically, her lips lifted at the corners in a bittersweet combination of contentment and sadness. Time together was well overdue.

But she would savor every moment with the best friend she had ever known. It would be like old times. A rare opportunity to relive a piece of their happy past, she reasoned. A guilty seed planted itself in Annie's chest. She didn't know why.

I'm not doing anything wrong; that's for sure. But I didn't tell Mamma where I was going. That's not like me. I don't intend to be sneaky. I've never hidden anything from my parents. And even though Levi's merely a friend, I figured they wouldn't want me to have much to do with him for fear our friendship might become something more. I don't want to alarm them; I don't think they ever understood what a huge hole in my life Levi's moving away left. Of course I didn't talk much about my sadness. What good would it have done? The circumstances couldn't be changed. I have to talk to him now. At the same time, I don't want to worry my folks. So . . . there's no perfect solution.

After all, Levi wasn't of their church. Not that she had joined yet. But she would when she was ready. In fact, she couldn't imagine going any other route.

Now here she was. She stopped a moment to catch her breath. Lifting her chin and squaring her shoulders, she proceeded up the hill with short, quick steps until she glimpsed the creek.

As the warm sun hit her shoulders, the air hinted of burning leaves. The thought reminded her that she had a lot to do in her own yard the moment she got home.

But that would have to wait. Because today she and Levi would both be at the very spot that, long ago, was their meeting place.

For that reason, Pebble Creek was quite special. Unique. Her times with Levi had been few and far between. As she glanced up at the bright sun, she blinked. For a moment, moisture blurred her vision at the thought of the happy occasions she and Levi had spent here. She smiled with satisfaction. Levi was an important part of her past.

A soft breeze nudged a single tendril of long hair loose from her covering. Automatically, she tucked it back underneath.

From a distance, she spotted Levi. Her heart pumped with excited happiness. She waved. He returned the friendly gesture and stepped quickly to meet her.

"It's good to see you, Annie."

"You too!" She didn't try to stop the excitement that edged her voice. "There's so much to catch up on."

He glanced toward the path alongside the creek. "Are you up for a walk?"

She offered an eager nod.

As they proceeded, Annie's pulse raced with a combination of excitement and happiness.

Automatically, she considered the unique person beside her. The boy she had looked up to. Now she had him all to herself. But only for a short time. She frowned. Soon Mamma would need her for chores.

How could she and Levi cover ten years in just an hour or so? Suddenly, she knew what she'd planned to accomplish was downright impossible. She looked up at him and giggled.

"What?"

She bumped into his side to avoid a dip in the earth. As soon as she regained her footing, she turned to him. "I was just wondering how fast the two of us could talk to cover a decade."

Offering an understanding nod, he smiled a little. "I know just what you mean. Hey . . ."

She looked up at him to continue.

"Maybe we should prioritize. You know, just touch on the important stuff."

She faced him and gave a strong shake of her head, resting a set of eager hands on her hips. Raising her chin, she looked him straight in the eye. "No prioritizing, Levi. I want to hear everything. Don't you dare leave out one detail!"

He pretended to check the silver watch on his left wrist. His voice feigned skepticism. "How much time have we got?"

She lowered her chin a notch. "An hour or so. Until I have to help with dinner."

As soon as she said the words, a sad rush swept through her, but she quickly ordered it away. There was only time for happiness. She didn't want to waste a second with him.

In a thoughtful silence, they traveled slightly up the lone hill. In front of them loomed Pebble Creek's main body. As if on cue, they sat down side by side.

"Our sitting stones are still here," she commented.

"I know. Remember when we carried them all the way from the creek?"

"*Jah!* They were so heavy; we brought them a few steps at a time, then put them down. Seemed like it took forever."

He nodded in agreement. "Now, ten years later, here we are." He gave a quick shrug of his shoulders. "I guess our efforts weren't wasted." He swallowed and lowered the pitch of his voice to a more serious tone. "I want to hear all about you."

She held up a hand of protest and lifted her chin. "Only after you tell me what you've been up to. Start with your family. How are they?"

"They're fine." Levi offered an amused nod. "That's my Annie. Always taking charge. You're every bit as direct and straightforward as when we were kids."

The green flecks on his pupils danced when a ray of sun hit them. "Just the way I like you."

She smiled a little. She bent her legs at the knees and hugged them, eyeing him with curiosity. "I'm serious. I'm dying to hear what you've been doing," she pressed. A giggle escaped her throat. "Let's call this our ten-year reunion."

"Okay. Then we'd better get talking."

"I can't believe you're back," she started. "Over the years . . ." Her gaze lowered to the ground before reconnecting with his. "I've wondered about you. I hoped with all my heart that life was kind to your family. I've prayed for God to take care of you."

He nodded appreciatively. When he looked at her, she took in his appearance. There was a new confidence about him. She guessed it had come with experience and age.

"That's so like you, Annie. Always thinking of others. But I've kept you in my prayers, too."

"Jah?"

He nodded. "Especially right after we left town." The corners of his lips dropped a couple of notches. "I had to make new friends, you know."

He adjusted his position on the rock. Taking a deep breath, he casually grabbed a stick near his foot and played with it while he spoke. "I'm sure you guessed our move wasn't without challenges."

Not sure what to say, she held his gaze.

"After we left, Dad basically started from scratch. I can't begin to tell you what we went through. Finding a place to live, him finding a job . . ." He let out a deep, agonizing sigh. "It was horrible."

She swallowed an emotional knot, quick to note his expression, a combination of regret and resentment.

"Levi . . ."

"The anger that I felt . , . I can't explain it. Like I said, I know Dad broke a rule, but the punishment was so . . . drastic. He drove his work truck." He paused before adding, "His driver quit and he had commitments, so he was forced to drive until he was able to replace him. It wasn't really Dad's fault."

Annie wanted to make things right for Levi and his family, but she couldn't. What had happened had been significant for her, too. A chapter with an unhappy ending, a denouement that couldn't be changed. John Miller's truck title was in his company's name. That was how the Amish did things. It wouldn't work to put a vehicle in the driver's name because it would mean that person could take off with it. Annie had been privy to that part of the Miller story.

Despite Annie's frustration, there wasn't anything she could do about the past. She shrugged her shoulders in defeat. "It was awful. But did your Dad try to make things right? Did he think of apologizing for what he did?"

The question seemed to take Levi off guard. His surprised raised brow made her catch her breath. Still, what she had asked didn't seem unreasonable to her.

"I'm not sure. What I do know is that he felt like his friends had abandoned him. It was no different from a cruel splash of cold water in the face. The hurt ran so deep, there was no way to fix it."

"If he had apologized . . ."

Levi raised a defensive hand to cut her off and gave a dismissive roll of his eyes. "Let's not go there, Annie. Because we'll never know."

A tear slid down Annie's cheek, but she stopped it.

"Hey," he whispered, "it's not your fault. No matter how hard you try, you can't control people. And as much as you try to change life, you can't. All you can do is react."

She blinked and accepted the truth. "It's not a perfect world."

He gave a slow shake of his head. "No. But you're here with me now. That makes it as perfect as it can be."

She smiled her relief and nodded. "No matter what happens, our friendship will always be."

He glanced away for a moment before looking back at her. "Our bond can never be broken. Promise?"

"Promise."

Annie's sad heart pounded with uncertainty. But time with Levi was precious. She thought of a more upbeat topic. "Your dad was lucky to have you. Even when we were kids, you always figured things out. You helped him build homes as far back as I can remember. Those skills must have come in handy."

"I'm his right-hand man," he said proudly. "At first, no one in the Morton area knew of him, so he did fix-ups."

She raised a curious brow.

"You know, remodeling kitchens and bathrooms and such. Lucky for us, there wasn't a lot of competition at the time. We finally got our break when a doctor and his wife liked the room we'd remodeled so much, they asked Dad to build a brand-new home for their daughter and husband-to-be."

It was quite common for the Amish to have their own businesses. Decades back, when land was cheap, most of them had farmed. But when land prices rose considerably, it became necessary to do other things.

He shrugged and offered a satisfied smile. "That was his big break, really. After that, his name and reputation spread quickly. We were able to move into a nicer, bigger place, and now we live in a two-story Dad and I built ourselves. And today . . . let's just say Dad paid his dues and enjoys the benefits of years of sacrifice. He pretty much picks and chooses his projects."

"Sounds like you're okay, then." She nodded approval and paused to think of the right words. "I'm so sorry, Levi. When I heard what happened, I couldn't believe it." She rolled her eyes in frustration. "It was a shock. And it weighed heavily on my mind for a long time."

His expression was a combination of appreciation and sympathy. "I wished I'd had the chance to at least say good-bye. But things; they happen so fast, it was like a blur. Suddenly, we left here. The only home I had ever known. Dad hired a driver to take us away. He led in his truck. Everything we took with us was stuffed in the two vehicles. Afterward, the house sold with no problem."

"I know."

He hesitated. Levi closed his eyes, as if every word was difficult to get out. Finally, he threw his arms to the sky, then dropped them to his thighs as he regarded her with a helpless expression on his face. "It was over, Annie. We quit the only life we knew. We moved on without anyone's help and survived."

The admission prompted her to lay back so her hands held her body up against the cold earth. "I don't know what to say. I wish I could have helped." Her voice cracked with emotion. "I would have done anything for your family."

He gave an understanding nod. "I know, Annie. You're a true friend. I'm telling you, don't even start to imagine what it's like to see the very people you love and work with . . . and depend on to suddenly treat you differently. When you're no longer one of them. Most in the community still spoke to him. But not everyone. But even those who did . . . their attitude?" He gave a shake of his head. "Could we have stayed? Of course. Some do. But it would never have been the same. It was easier to move to a strange place than to stay where everyone knew you were no longer one of them."

Before she could offer her opinion, he held up a defensive hand. "I'm fully aware that the *Ordnung* doesn't allow for deviation. The rules are etched in stone. You can't erase them. Or edit them. And, obviously, Dad broke one. But . . ."

A long silence ensued while he closed his eyes. When a lone tear slid down his cheek, salty tears stung Annie's own eyes, and regret encompassed her heart and soul. If only John Miller hadn't crossed the line. If only the rules weren't so strict. If only she could undo the past for Levi, she would. Why on earth did it have to be this way?

His voice softened, "I know what you're thinking in that busy head of yours."

"You do?" She raised a challenging brow. "Okay, enlighten me."

He pressed his lips together. "When we were kids, you always prayed for everyone to get along. You longed for a perfect world. I've always thought of you as a dreamer."

She smiled.

"And even though we've been apart a decade, that doesn't change anything, Annie. Because I still know your heart. You want every story to have a happy ending."

She gave a slow nod of agreement. He was right.

He leaned forward. He was so close, his warm breath feathered her eyelashes.

She didn't move. "You know me better than anyone, Levi. It's like . . ." She thought for a moment. "It's as if you can read my mind. And I'm *not* happy when things aren't right. I *do* like happy endings. For every situation. Mamma always tells me something good will come out of something bad. And the truth is . . ." She stood and walked in the direction of Pebble Creek.

When she turned, he was right behind her. She looked up and breathed a hopeful sigh. "We're here for such a short time. And I've always been taught that God supports forgiveness and love. Of course I want things to be right. Especially for your family."

She drew her hands over her chest and closed her

eyes in a plea that must give away everything she felt. "Levi, I would be lying if I said I didn't want things to be the way they used to be." She pressed both sets of fingers together so hard, her knuckles popped. "I pray for it. And I'll never give up. In my heart of hearts . . . something good *will* come out of this. I know it."

She dropped her arms to her sides and lowered her voice. "I don't want you to leave. Ever. But only God knows what will happen in the end, and we have to go through setbacks to get there. It's really hard to be patient."

She eyed Levi for a response. To her disappointment, he merely looked away. Together, slow steps took them back to their spots. But her mind flitted in every direction. She'd had her say.

Mamma always told her to keep some things to herself. That people didn't need to know her every thought. But that was Annie's way. She was a straight shooter.

She couldn't bear the thought of losing her best friend again. He was like her partner. The person she needed beside her to be complete. She wasn't sure why this feeling was suddenly more powerful than ever; she only knew her emotions were so strong and frustration came at her from every direction.

With one desperate moment to try to make things better, she added, "Levi, I've always been taught at church that God has a plan for each of us. In fact, Old Sam brings it up all the time."

Before he could respond, his grin brought a smile

to her face. "Sometimes we don't understand why things happen. Especially, if they hurt us."

She paused for effect, and he nodded with understanding.

She drew in a thoughtful breath and held his eyes. "At times, it might seem like things are falling apart. It's easy to give up. To let the bad get the best of us. But we can't let go of hope, Levi. God rewards the faithful." She softened her voice. "I strongly believe that."

A cool breeze caressed the back of her neck as she continued. "We only know what's happening at the moment. We can't help it because we're human. But God is fully aware of our every step. And that includes what happens in the end and all we go through, good and bad. So, Levi, your dad's story and ours must have happy endings."

She pressed her lips together. "Promise me you believe it, too. And that you'll keep your faith."

She took in his expression, which was a combination of surprise and confusion.

"You really believe that, don't you?"

Pressing her lips together, she nodded. "I *know* it."

He gave a quick, uncertain shake of his head. "You're amazing, my Annie. Your faith is so convincing. Honestly, I don't know where you get it. Truth is, I don't think I measure up to what God wants me to be. I wish I believed like you."

"I'm sure you do, Levi. But sometimes we struggle. Because God tests us."

She wondered if she made sense and decided to give him an example. "Think of the disciples.

What they went through. Their lives were filled with setback after setback. How easy it would have been for them to quit. But they didn't. They persevered. As far as your family goes, the shunning . . . it was awful."

She hesitated before continuing.

"And don't ask me why things happened like they did, but it had to be a part of God's greater plan."

More than ever, she yearned to convince him. She looked intently into his eyes. But the expression she glimpsed there was troubled. This made her even more determined to get through to him.

She paused to choose the right words. "Right now, we're mortal. We try to make sense of it all, but we can't. I mean, that's impossible. But when we're in heaven with our families, everything will be crystal clear. In fact, we'll probably wonder why we worried so much."

She eyed him for a reaction. Finally, he cupped his chin with his hand. "Annie, there's something I've got to tell you."

She eyed him with curiosity.

"In all the years I've been away, I've made new friends. But no one matches you." He leaned closer and whispered, "You're special."

For long special moments, she processed what he'd just said. Her heart fluttered in delight.

She drew her hands to her chest in a combination of surprise and gratitude. And when she responded, she couldn't control the breathlessness in her voice. "Thank you, Levi. I'll never forget that." She cleared her throat; still, her voice cracked with sentiment.

"It's planted in my mind like a seed. It will be a part of our friendship that will stay with me forever."

Not wanting to become too emotional during their limited time together, she tried to slow the excited beat of her heart to a calmer pace. For some time they sat side by side and gazed at Pebble Creek.

"Do you believe how serious we are?"

They laughed.

"I know!" He waggled a hand in the air. "That only reinforces that we've been apart too long." He offered a friendly nudge.

Automatically, she forced the subject to something less personal. "I'm curious."

"About what?"

"Do you have hobbies?"

The mood changed with a snap of two fingers and she breathed a sigh of relief as he faced her. "You won't believe this."

"Try me," she teased.

"I'm a volunteer fireman."

She straightened up with new excitement. "*Jah?*"

He gave a proud nod.

She thought for a moment. "Of course you are. How could I forget?"

"What?"

She widened her eyes in sudden recollection. "When we were kids, you were fascinated with rescue workers. I'll never forget when Old Sam's shed burned and the firemen showed up. You were only this high." She estimated with her fingers above the ground. "And you were in awe of the guys who jumped out of that big red truck. Everyone around was concerned about the fire, but you were intrigued by the hoses. You asked all sorts of questions." She giggled. "One of the men even gave you his hat to try on."

He joined her in laughter. "I won't deny it. And my fascination stayed. When I got older, I read every book I could about firemen. It just so happened a small town near us asked for volunteers."

"And of course you signed up."

"Yup. I went through training." He eyed her from his peripheral vision. "It was pretty tough."

"How many fires have you put out?"

"So far, two."

She nodded approval. "There's not a better way to help your community."

"There's way more to it than serving, Annie. It's rewarding." He touched a proud fist to his chest. "You can't put a price tag on hearing the relief in a father's voice after we pull his son from a second-story house. Or the excited look on a widow's face when we rescue her cat. It's really something to make such a contribution to people's lives."

He raised an uncertain brow. "I'm thinking seriously about what you said about God's plan for us, and that every step, good and bad, leads to the final result. And it makes sense. My parents' expectations have changed since we moved away."

He took a deep breath and leaned closer. "Right now I'm torn. I'm at a place in the road where I don't know my next move. Since high school graduation my folks have wanted me to go to college." He gave a casual shrug of his shoulders. "I understand why they'd want that. But wouldn't it be a waste of time and money if I'm not sure what I want to do?"

"Maybe."

"I struggle to figure out my purpose in life. But to tell the truth, I'm not sure what it is. And when I put pressure on myself to decide, I only get stressed."

Her heart warmed at his honesty. "Maybe you're trying too hard. Maybe . . ." She shrugged. "It will come to you if you don't worry about it. Pray about it, Levi. Then you'll know. Maybe not tomorrow. Or the next day. Be patient."

A happy giggle escaped her as she stood. He got up at the same time.

"Why, just look at you. The world's at your doorstep. You're healthy. You've got both arms and legs. And there's not a doubt in my mind you can do whatever you set out to. But surely it's gonna take time to decide what that is. It's not as easy as knowing what to have for dinner. Or what time to get up in the morning."

He nodded agreement. "You're right."

They took a few steps. His expression became more subdued. It reminded her of the calm after a big thunderstorm. Those interesting flecks in his eyes stopped dancing and eventually disappeared. The excited edge in his voice went away. "You know, that's what I miss most about you, I think."

"What?"

"Your confidence in me."

She squared her shoulders. "I've always believed in you. That'll never change."

He nodded appreciatively. "I remember when we were kids, I never worried about anything really.

Because you were always my cheerleader." As if feeling the need to explain, he darted her a wry smile. "You know, sports teams always have the girls on the sideline who root for them? And what's cool is that they clap even if you're down."

He lowered his tone to a more emotional pitch. "That's what you do for me."

Annie pressed her lips together thoughtfully. "How could I not believe in you?"

She considered what he'd said about college. In a way, she wished her own path was as open as his. She would like to have the opportunity to do whatever she wanted. But Amish girls were pretty much expected to marry early, raise a family, and help support their husband's career by doing bookwork and such. Her life had already been planned for her to an extent really. But that was okay. She wanted to follow that likely path. What the church and her parents expected. Still, to her dismay, a tinge of envy swept through her. She wasn't proud of this unusual sensation. She would have to pray to rid herself of it.

Why did she suddenly feel jealous of Levi for being able to choose his occupation? The question nagged at her.

She'd started teaching after the eighth grade. As far as education went, he was mountains ahead of her. But that didn't matter. They'd always had mutual respect. Something unconditional. He'd never tried to change her and never would. Since Levi had left, she hadn't replaced him. She couldn't begin to.

They reclaimed their stones. "Have you ever

thought of working with your dad as a career?" she asked.

Levi leaned back a notch, dug his fingers deep into his jeans pockets, and hooked his thumbs over the tops. "Yup. Still do. I think he'd like that. Dad and I get along well. But right now, my future's up in the air."

He paused, then said, "Annie, I hope God will show me my path. I pray every night for guidance. Whatever choices I make now could affect the rest of my life." He shrugged. "I'm sure if I'm going to spend time working, I want to do something I love. When I'm old, I'd like to be able to say I've enjoyed my life. How about you?"

When he looked at her, she felt her cheeks flush. She wasn't sure why, and silently scolded herself.

"You're blushing!"

She rolled her eyes. "No, I'm not."

He hesitated. "It's nothing to be ashamed of, Annie. I used to love that about you. I'd even tease you just to watch your cheeks redden. And . . ."

"What?"

He grinned sheepishly.

She crossed her arms over her breasts and sat up straighter. "You liked that I blushed?"

He nodded.

"When did I turn red?"

"All the time! I don't think there's anything you can do about it. Not that you should. The color's becoming to you. Think of how fortunate you are." He winked. "English girls spend money on makeup to get that look, but you've got an advantage over them. I think God made you with a built-in shade of reddish-pink. Consider it a gift."

A laugh that was a combination of surprise and happiness escaped her, and he joined in.

Annie wished she could stay there and talk forever. Whatever she said, Levi supported her.

"Remember when Old Sam and Esther let us keep that kitten in his barn?"

Levi leaned back onto the stone and crossed his ankles, biting on a clover he'd pulled from a patch as he spoke. "I'd forgotten. But now it's coming back." He snapped his fingers. "Autumn, we called her. I remember the day we found that little bit of a thing by the creek, all lost and alone. She clung to us like we were parents. We couldn't decide who should keep her, so we shared her."

"I'll never forget her silky hair. And it was an unusual shade of brown."

"Like leaves in the fall."

"That's why we called her Autumn. We took her to Old Sam and asked if we could keep her in his barn. Of course he let us. I think Esther fed her as well." Levi shook his head. "There'll never be another Esther; that's for sure." He lifted an inquisitive chin. "Whatever happened to Autumn?"

Annie gave a reluctant shrug. "She left the barn at night. Sam fed her at sunrise. One morning he waited for her, but she didn't come back."

He gave a sad shake of his head. "Do you have any pets?"

"I'd like another kitten, but right now Mamma says we have enough to take care of with the cattle and horses. How about you?"

"I have a golden retriever. After we moved, we adopted her from the Humane Society." He swallowed.

Annie was fully aware that the shunning didn't prompt happy memories. Yet she yearned to know about his life.

"I think it was compensation for taking me away from you." He rolled his eyes.

She drew in a happy breath. "Really?"

"Yup." A long silence passed between them. Then he said, "It wouldn't be a good reunion without a walk to the end of the property."

They stood at the same time. As they walked alongside Pebble Creek, they threw small stones into the shallow water to see who could make the bigger splash.

Levi's voice was soft. "By the way, I've been wondering: Did you ever make it to Six Flags? Our English buddies used to tell us about the rides. You always wanted to go. We talked about it and planned to do it during *Rumspringa.*"

Annie smiled a little.

"So did you make it there, Ms. Mast?"

She paused at the way he'd addressed her. When she spoke, it was in a more serious tone. "Why on earth would I go without you? It wouldn't have been fun."

As he walked her to the end of the property, she told him what she'd done the past decade. About learning to make sponge cakes, her relationship with Old Sam, and her coveted role as a teacher. She went on to tell him that the girls her age didn't much interest her and about her goal to become the mother of lots of happy children.

Not long after that, they said good-bye, and Annie continued home. She had spent the most perfect day of her life with Levi, but now her heart sank. There was no confidant like him. Not even Old Sam. She knew she could be happy the rest of her days spending every afternoon at Pebble Creek with Levi Miller. He had returned. And she wished more than anything he could stay.

Chapter Three

Jake was waiting at the front door. When Levi stepped inside, the little guy looked up at him with wide, hopeful eyes. Even in October, he was barefoot; his pant legs were rolled up, revealing a small set of shins. His dark suspenders looked a size too large against the boy's narrow shoulders.

The picture in front of Levi prompted a laugh.

Remembering his manners, he looked into the kitchen and waved. "Good afternoon, Aunt Abigail."

At the gas stove, she offered a slight nod. "Levi. Sure is nice out there."

"Can we go feed the squirrels?"

Jake's pressing tone didn't surprise Levi. Animals were the little boy's favorite pastime.

Levi nodded toward the boy's mother. "Better ask your mom."

Automatically, the two glanced at the woman stirring what smelled like cream of celery soup. Raising a dark brow that was a combination of skepticism and amusement, she nodded and smiled. A dismissive hand followed. "Go on. But make it fast. Supper's almost ready."

Outside, the barefoot boy led Levi to the side door of the old barn and pointed up to a shelf of dried corn ears. Levi glanced around at the bales of hay stacked neatly on the far wall, extending up to the roof. Most of the building was cordoned off for cattle.

Happy memories flooded his mind as he continued to absorb the ambience. Brown containers of grain loomed in the distance. Levi breathed in the old familiar scent of the farm and smiled a little. He knew that to his English friends the smell would be revolting. But to him, for some strange reason, it sent a comforting, familiar sensation through his entire body.

Little Jake interrupted his thoughts, nudging his arm and pointing to a shelf with his free hand.

With a swift motion, Levi easily reached for an ear of corn and handed it to the kid.

"Denke."

Without responding, Levi pulled another one from the pile. Looking down at the wide, eager eyes, he said, "One for you and one for me. Deal?"

Jake's grin was endearing. The boy's eyes beamed with joy. *"Jah."*

Outside, quick, impatient steps took the boy to the family well. Levi followed. The Miller family was one of the few in the area that didn't use city water. The copper pump stood in the middle of a large, circular concrete slab. Standing on the edge, Levi helped Jake shuck the corn and let the yellow seeds drop.

The breeze caressed the kernels and pushed them away from the well. As if on cue, two brown squirrels appeared. They stopped to stand on their hind feet, as if they deliberated whether to come forward. Levi stood perfectly still. So did Jake.

A long silence ensued while the squirrels studied the food with keen interest. Finally, one after the other, they stole some kernels and ran away. In the distance, three other squirrels contemplated their options. While they did so, from out of nowhere, another moved forward.

This animal was at least a size smaller than the others. The white patch on his head made him easy to identify. He proceeded to Jake's feet and grabbed a kernel. But to Levi's surprise, the creature didn't rush away; instead, he lingered and ate at his leisure.

Jake laughed and pointed. "He's mine." With a slow, steady motion, the boy bent to pet the squirrel on the head. More to Levi's amazement, the animal looked up at Jake and chattered. Obviously, the two were friends. The creature was obviously tame.

The amusing interaction between animal and child continued. Levi smiled at the pair. "What's his name?"

Jake glanced at Levi and shrugged. "I don't know."

Levi raised his brow. "You mean he doesn't have one?"

Only appearing interested in the small creature that chattered without stop, Jake didn't respond. But Levi persisted. "Jake, if he's your pet, you have to call him something. Otherwise, he won't feel special."

As soon as the words came out, Levi realized how

ridiculous he sounded, but after all, he was talking to a five-year-old.

Jake handed his corn to Levi to shuck it.

"Levi! Jake! Suppertime!"

The two glanced at each other. With an encouraging nod, Levi motioned to the squirrel. "Time to say good-bye to your friend." But when Jake turned, the small animal had disappeared.

Levi wrapped an affectionate arm around the youngster. "Come on. Your mamma's waiting for us."

On the way to the house, Levi threw his shucked ear in the dumpster. The half-finished corn remained on the ground.

Inside, the enticing aroma of cream of celery soup prompted Levi to lick his lips. It was his favorite. And, to his benefit, Aunt Abigail's was the world's best. His stomach growled as he and Jake hung their coats on their respective hooks. Jake's was closer to the floor.

"Did you think of a name?"

All smiles, Jake looked up. "Friend."

Levi chuckled.

After supper, Levi bonded with Jake until bedtime. When his little hand was in Levi's large one, a strange, wonderful sensation swept up Levi's arms. He reasoned it was from all the unconditional love Jake gave him. His little cousin reminded him of himself at that age. Trusting. Loving. And the way Jake looked at him melted Levi's heart.

Levi recalled his own childhood. He didn't have to try hard to remember his strong trust in Annie. Although he had protected her, she, in turn, had been his security blanket. She'd looked out for him, too, with a motherly affection. He grinned. Her smallness hadn't made her any less protective and nurturing.

And he'd never forget leaving town. As he and his folks had pulled away with their driver, wondering how they were going to start over again in a new place, he had yearned to talk to his best friend. He hadn't known how she could help to make things better; yet he'd been sure she could. Unfortunately, that opportunity hadn't presented itself.

He'd begged his folks to let him say good-bye to Annie. His dad's answer hadn't left negotiating room. Levi closed his eyes and breathed in a painful sigh, knowing he would never, ever forget the huge loss that had continually haunted him, even after they'd settled into their small apartment.

A voice pulled him back to the present. The barefoot kid looked up at Levi. "Will you pray with me?"

Surprised, Levi nodded. As he knelt beside Jake on the hardwood floor, a strange emotion tugged at his heart. The soft voice began, "Dear God, thank You for *Maem*, *Daed*, Aidan, Elijah, Friend, and Levi." The boy's voice was soft and sincere. "Please don't let Levi go home. I want him here with me. Amen."

The last sentence tugged at Levi's heart until his chest ached. He swallowed a knot of emotion and tucked the boy in. He took in the innocent face that stared up at him with great admiration. Long eyelashes. Small feet sticking out of the covers. The scene in front of him was nothing less than beautiful.

As soon as Jake closed his eyes, Levi considered what Annie had said about God's plan. About all the steps, good and bad, along the way taking us to the end result. He didn't know if it was true; it certainly made sense. And it made him feel a heck of a lot better because he didn't yet know his life's purpose.

He stepped away, not taking his eyes off the rising and falling of the cover over Jake's chest. The boy's lips were parted. Levi wondered what it would be like to be Jake. Not to have a care in the world other than feeding his squirrel.

He dug his hands into the pockets of his jeans, wondering if God had brought him back to be little Jake's role model.

Not wanting to leave the room, he quietly took a seat in the wooden rocking chair in the corner. As he watched Jake sleep, his conversation with Annie crept into his mind and settled there. He couldn't stop thinking of Annie's view of God's plan. That life was a series of steps, and that they couldn't all be good ones. But the setbacks, as well as golden moments, were necessary to reach God's desired ending for each of us. Salty tears stung his eyes and he blinked. He wasn't sure of the reason for his tears. He wasn't sad. On the contrary, he was drifting back to his happy Amish childhood. Like Jake, Levi had been protected by his family and their tight-knit community.

The union of people supporting him had been kind of like a protective shield. He'd never feared a thing. At that time, he'd had very little but had never felt deprived because what he'd had was all the love a kid could want. He'd had everything. At night he'd gone to sleep in a bed that had been hand-made by his father, in an austere room just like this one. His closet hadn't been full of tennis shoes like now. But his mother had made the deep blue curtains that covered most of his bedroom windows. And his mom had knelt each night to say his prayers with him. She'd also made the soft, warm quilt he'd pulled up over his body.

Levi pressed his lips together in deep deliberation. More than ever, he felt God sending him a message. Yet he still wasn't sure. *How can I be getting a signal if I don't know what it is?*

With calm certainty, Annie had assured him that God would lead him to take the right steps, even though right now he didn't know what they were. Their conversation had been simple, yet her words had renewed his faith. And his strength.

More than ever, Levi was determined to learn God's purpose for him. The most important reason he'd been put here on the earth. If God had an important job for everyone, what was his?

As he drew in a sigh, he stood and took one last look at Jake. Levi hadn't done anything to deserve the kid's unconditional admiration. Jake's chest rose and fell, and Levi took in the innocent face. It was amazing that God had created this special boy who had won Levi's heart. An unexpected rush of love filled him. He continued to search his soul for the reason God had brought him back to this community. In desperation, he squeezed his eyes closed and pressed his palms together. He whispered, "Dear God, I know I'm here for a reason. Please tell me what it is."

* * *

Annie stepped up to the front door. She'd spent more time at Pebble Creek that afternoon than she'd planned on. The moment she was inside, Mamma eyed her with a combination of curiosity and disapproval.

Pretending to ignore the look of disfavor, Annie hung her coat on the hook and quickly proceeded to wash her hands. "Sorry I'm late, Mamma," she hollered from the bathroom. "I'll help with supper as soon as I wash up."

Annie's heart pumped to a hard, nervous beat as she rushed to complete her task as her conversation with Levi flooded her mind with unanswered questions. Right now she'd have to put them on the back-burner.

Mamma was unhappy. Annie could tell by the dismayed expression on her face. By the way her brows furrowed in skepticism. By the not-so-warm tone of her voice.

Without wasting time, Annie stepped with forced enthusiasm to the utensil drawer and pulled out the forks and spoons. As she did so, Mamma stood next to her, breathing a deep sigh of frustration. "I don't suppose I need to ask where you've been."

Now Annie knew what this was all about. Somehow Mamma was fully aware of Annie's time with Levi. Meeting her gaze, Annie lifted a proud chin. She'd always been honest and direct, and this time wouldn't be an exception. "I was with Levi, Mamma. At Pebble Creek. I wasn't trying to be sneaky. I just didn't want you to worry."

Not encouraging further discussion, Annie stepped to the table. As she carefully placed utensils to the side of creamy white plates, a long, tense silence ensued. Annie frowned and contemplated the unexpected tension. She had hoped to keep her visit with Levi a secret. There was no use upsetting her parents, but moments with Levi couldn't wait.

Without a doubt, Mamma disapproved of their time together, even though Annie had done nothing wrong. She wasn't sure why her mother felt this dissatisfaction. In Annie's opinion, *wrong* was what her own community had done to Levi's father. If blame was to be placed, they should share it equally with John Miller.

"Need I ask what you two were up to?"

Annie stopped what she was doing, took a deep, decisive breath, and moved confidently to her mamma, who had removed a large foil piece off the pot roast. Breathing in the delicious scent, Mamma stirred a pot of ham and bean soup. Annie looped an affectionate arm around Mamma's neck and planted a reassuring kiss on her cheek. In her softest, most reassuring voice, she pleaded, "Mamma, please don't worry. Surely Levi and I can catch up on things."

She sighed. "He won't be here long."

Annie gave a defensive shrug. "He's the best friend I ever had. It's just not fair."

Frowning, Mamma raised the pitch of her voice a notch. "Honey, you don't have to remind me of your friendship. I'm sure everyone around here remembers that you two were inseparable." She turned to Annie, the expression on her face a combination of pleading and desperation. "But, honey, that was ten years ago. You were kids. He was good for you then. And nothing was wrong with it at the time."

Annie put her hands on her hips and lifted her chin. "Nothing's wrong with it *now*, Mamma."

Her mother didn't respond immediately. Finally, when she did, her shoulders had sagged. "Maybe not. But things are different now, Annie."

Annie lifted a brow in protest. "Really? How?" The last thing she wanted was a confrontation, but this one seemed inevitable. She watched Mamma's brows draw together as she studied the ingredients in the oversize pot as if it was a map of the world. Finally, Mamma lowered her voice to a more understanding tone. She put the stirring spoon on a dish towel and pulled Annie to stand at arm's length.

"You're of courtin' age. And Levi's not in our church. Everything between you two might seem innocent . . ."

"It *is*! How can you . . ."

Annie couldn't finish her question because her mother jumped in. "Honey, you're missing the point. I trust you. And it seems as though Levi has grown up into a nice young man. But I don't have to remind you how fast word travels around here. Can you imagine what everyone might think?" She waved a dismissive hand. "It would bring shame to our whole family if people started talking."

Annie's jaw dropped in shock as Mamma's words registered. Annie couldn't believe what she'd just heard. For several moments she stood with her mouth open. "Mamma?"

She waited for Annie to continue.

"You've always been fair. Surely you're not telling me to stay away from Levi. I can't do that. We've already been pulled apart. I won't let it happen again."

While she ordered herself to stay composed, her voice shook with emotion. Tears streamed down her face. "I prayed for him and his family for ten years. All that time, I wondered if he was okay. What he was doing. If his father had landed on his feet." She caught her breath. "Finally, Levi and I got to talk, thanks to the wedding he almost didn't come to. But, Mamma, he's not going to stay." Annie almost choked on her words. "He's leaving. And until that happens I want to spend every moment I can with him."

She watched as the look on Mamma's face filled with even more desperation. When they faced each other again, Annie thought she detected fear in the low tone of her mother's voice. "Annie, I wish I could make you understand. I don't mean to underestimate the strong bond you two share. Lots of children never forget who they played with when they were little."

"It's more than that, Mamma."

Mamma's voice tensed. "You can't have a future with Levi. At some point you've got to admit it."

Annie's jaw dropped. At first she didn't respond, considering the dismal words. Her mother's directness had surprised her. Finally, she lowered her eyes to the floor. Her own voice sounded tired and discouraged. "You don't have to tell me there's no future with him. I know it. And I haven't even considered it. But our friendship . . . it's real. Despite what happened, he came back. Over the years, he's had to recover. And he's trying to forgive and forget. To be honest, he's a better person than me. I don't know how he even looks at some of these people after what they did to his daddy."

Mamma put a firm hand on her hip. "Annie, don't you talk like that. John Miller was fully aware of his actions. And by the way, that wasn't the first time he'd done what he wanted. Do you think he didn't know he was breaking the rules?"

Annie shook her head.

Mamma nodded her approval. "Of course he knew what he was doing."

"Mamma, it was only one thing. I'm not condoning what he did. I know he drove his truck when his driver quit. I just don't understand why we had to ruin his whole life."

"Honey, shunning brings sadness to the whole church. When John was baptized into the church, he agreed to abide by its guidelines. Disobedience to something you promise to uphold is a sin. According to the Bible, shunning is required by the other members."

Annie lowered her chin a notch.

"He brought this on himself, Annie. Don't go blaming us." She cleared her throat. "I don't want to hear any more about how badly we treated him. He could have resolved that whole mess if he'd apologized and hired another driver. The community would have taken him back."

Annie thought for a moment. Finally, she shrugged. "Maybe. Maybe not. What's done is done. It's not a perfect world, Mamma. Isn't that what forgiveness is all about? I just don't see why life can't continue in a kinder manner. And as far as Levi goes, he's honest. Decent. One of the best. If everyone around here looks at Levi as the son of a man who was shunned, that's hardly fair. He shouldn't suffer the consequences of his father."

"But that's not the case, Annie. We all know what a fine young man Levi is. No one's arguing that. But . . ."

Annie took her mamma's shoulders between two firm palms. "Mamma, listen to me. There's nothing to worry about. This conversation's a waste of time. You trust me, don't you?"

Mamma nodded without hesitation.

"Then hear me out. I don't know how I can make you understand . . . what I feel for Levi . . . it's rare. I believe in him with everything I say and do. What we built years ago . . . it's too strong to just wave it good-bye. Levi believes in the Lord, just like me. And nothing he did is cause for me to ignore him. If people talk, I'm sorry. Maybe they should pray harder to mind their own business."

"Annie!"

"It's true, Mamma. This is ridiculous. I've always tried to please you and Dad. But you have to understand that there's nothing in this world that will stop me from being his friend."

That evening, slow, uncertain steps took Annie toward her hope chest. She stood for long moments to admire the carved recipe before raising the lid. With a deep sigh, she bent down to take out her journal. As always, she left the gift from Old Sam open to view the beautiful deep blue velvet lining.

A moonbeam zoomed in through the window, landing on a spot on the floor just in front of her bed. As she sat in the middle of the circle of light, she pulled a lantern closer for even more light.

She entered the date on her journal, hesitated, and studied the otherwise blank page. There was so much to write about. And even more to figure out. The thoughts flitting through her mind weren't connecting and she wasn't sure where to start.

"Okay," she decided. "May as well begin with the afternoon at Pebble Creek." Trying to make sense of everything, she dropped the journal to her lap and pressed her fingers against her cheeks. For a moment she closed her eyes and tried to focus. An uncertain sensation swept dangerously up her arms to her shoulders. Automatically, she rolled them to rid herself of the tingle.

As her conversation with Levi replayed in her mind, she started to write.

I treasure my time with Levi. I expected to cover the entire past ten years; that hardly happened. The focus ended up being on his dad's shunning. How it had affected the Millers and how Levi feels about it.

She frowned.

Part of him hasn't recovered. He didn't say it, but I know. Maybe he never will. I wouldn't want to be in his shoes. On the other hand, I might.

She bit her lip and considered her last words. It certainly didn't make her feel good.

I don't know why, but when Levi explained his options, I wondered what it would be like to have them. When I responded that the world was at his doorstep, I meant it. But that confession made me realize that the difference between us is much larger than our faith.

She paused to cross her hands over her lap. She didn't like the fact that their paths were so unalike. His seemed to branch off in many routes while hers proceeded in one predictable direction. She continued to write.

I may have told a lie. I'm not sure. I confessed to Mamma that I didn't want anything but friendship with Levi.

Her heart jumped to a dangerous, uncertain beat. Annie put down the pen and journal, stood, and went to the window. Her conversation with Mamma floated through her mind. So did the one she'd had with Levi.

What I said to my mother . . . it was wrong. It was rude. I didn't mean to hurt her or seem disrespectful. If Levi weren't so important to me, I wouldn't pursue our friendship. I'd spare Mamma the pain and keep quiet. But Levi is important to me. And I feel responsible for what his family went through. I've been raised to follow the Ordnung. *But in my mind, I long for adventure. The unexpected. As I get older, I realize the strict rules we commit to when we join the church. And I understand that shunning is sometimes necessary. But it makes me sad. I'm certainly not without flaw. It's not a perfect world, and we are human.*

While she contemplated the impact John Miller's shunning had had on everyone around him, including her family and Levi's, she wondered if the punishment was much worse than the sin. She wasn't sure. Maybe when she got older she would know. As she looked into the night, she took in the star-cluttered sky.

If God can create something so amazing, He could work out a way not to shun Levi's dad. I can't let that bother me so much. Because it's out of my control. If I could set the rules, there would be no shunning. Unless the sin was murder.

As the aroma of homemade butter filled the room, Annie rested her back against her bed and adjusted her journal.

There's something else I'm uneasy about.

She fidgeted with her hands, then moved her feet to a more comfortable position. The conversation with Mamma replayed in her head until Annie's temples pounded. She closed her eyes. When she opened them again, she returned pen to paper.

Mamma said I could never have a future with Levi. Of course I know that. For some reason, though, that thought is unsettling. I'm not sure why.

She pressed her lips together in deep thought, then continued.

Why can't Mamma trust me? I've tried to do right by my parents. And to my faith. I've never given them reason to doubt my actions. They've always believed in me. So why would they want to deprive me of the best friend I've ever had? And what have I done to make them doubt me?

Chapter Four

The following morning the bright October sun gracefully floated in through the opened doors of Old Sam's barn. Wearing dark suspenders and a long-sleeved shirt Sam had rolled up at the wrists, he etched a flower garden into a beautiful raw piece of cherry.

Annie wondered if this hope chest was for Rachel. Sam had already made one for her and Rebecca. Annie studied the intent expression on his face with keen interest. His gray beard had traces of white. Whenever Sam contemplated an issue, he ran his fingers through the long hair. She knew him like the back of her small, freckled hand. His weathered visage was lined with wrinkles; he always joked that his face was a map of his life, and that each line represented a significant blessing.

Today, Sam was hers. Sometimes she had to share him with Rebecca and Rachel. She didn't mind. In fact, she was happy the other two also doted on him. After all, she couldn't spend every minute with him. Besides, Sam lived by himself. He surely got lonely in his big old house. Thank goodness for faithful Buddy, his dog.

Annie wanted to make sure Sam had all the love and kindness he deserved. They were things you could never have too much of. Annie knew God had a plan for everyone, but she still thought it sad that Sam had outlived his two sons. And that he'd lost his wife to pneumonia. Still, his faith was strong.

His work never ceased to amaze her. He was a unique talent. There weren't many in the Plain Faith who hadn't heard of hope chest maker Sam Beachy. In fact, his artistic designs had made him a sort of celebrity. And to think he'd made a special chest just for her. The gift she kept by her bed was her rarest treasure. Sometimes she would just stand over it, admiring the beautiful sponge cake recipe.

As she watched him work, wood chippings dropped to the concrete floor. The woodsy smell filled her nostrils with delight. There was something so nice and homey about the scent. It was just like the way the air smelled after grass was mowed. It was incredible what art could come from a simple piece of wood. Old Sam created magic with his large, skilled hands.

Annie trusted him. Loved him. She heeded his advice. He was wiser than anyone she knew. Not many were fortunate enough to have such a friend.

It was moments like these that she loved most. The times she watched Old Sam create works of genius to make others happy. While he did his work, she allowed her mind to wander to a faraway dreamland she shared only with him.

His leathered, wrinkled hand held his designer

knife with great steadiness as he carefully carved. From time to time he paused and pressed his lips together in deep concentration. The lines around his eyes deepened as he bent closer to the board. Crinkles outlined the clear brown depths.

"Who's this one for?" Annie sat next to him in the special wooden rocking chair he'd made just for her, with Sam's Irish setter at her feet. Buddy rested happily against Annie's black shoes, gazing up at her from time to time. The dog loved attention. Annie bent to plant an affectionate kiss on his reddish hair. In response, Buddy offered a grateful whimper.

Finally, Sam put down his knife and turned to Annie with a sigh. "This one's for a Seattle woman who learned about me from a website set up by an English lady." Sam cleared a knot from his throat and dusted the area around his work with long, artistic fingers. He took his own seat next to Annie and continued. "It a sad story actually."

"Why?"

"The woman's name is Elaine. She was diagnosed with stage four lung cancer." A sad shake of his head followed.

Annie's chest ached at the thought. "That's terrible."

Sam nodded. "She's not expected to live much longer, so she's collecting her most special treasures to put in the chest I'm making for her daughter to pass down to her children. Elaine's hoping to see her daughter married."

Annie blinked back a salty tear. "That's a sweet

story. But I'm still sad that her child won't have a mamma. Do you know the girl's name?"

Sam paused, rubbing Buddy's back with his shoe. "Patricia."

"Patricia must be devastated."

The thought prompted an uncomfortable feeling in Annie's stomach, and she wrapped her hands around her waist. "I mean, she'll have a husband but not a mamma. I don't know what I would do without mine."

Sam's gentle eyes met her gaze. As he rocked back and forth, his voice was comforting, as always. "We're each planted here on this earth to carry out a mission for God. And we leave on His time." Sam sat back in his chair.

"I wish I could talk to God to ask Him why He does some things. It would seem like Elaine's purpose would be to be a good grandmamma to Patricia's children." She hesitated. "Nothing's more important than being a mamma or grandmamma."

Sam eyed her in understanding.

"Why would God take Patricia's mamma from her when she's so young? It's not fair."

Sam smiled a little. He had a way of making her feel everything would be okay because God would make sure of it. Even so, Annie still wondered why Patricia had to lose her mother so soon.

"Little one, God's plan is His choosing." He paused, a thoughtful expression crossing his face as he seemed to drift away. Annie straightened, wondering if he was thinking about Esther. Annie was sure she was in heaven. In fact, she was probably busy making sponge cakes for everyone. She had been well-known throughout the community for her home cooking, and after she passed on, Annie had continued making her delicious desserts so Old Sam wouldn't go hungry. He loved those cakes. Good thing Annie had learned to make them. But it had taken several attempts to get them the right texture.

Sam's voice was soft. "One of my favorite proverbs goes like this: The person who sews seeds of kindness enjoys perpetual harvest." He cleared his throat. "I imagine Patricia knows in her heart that her mother will finish reaping that harvest in heaven. And it's that very realization that will get her through her loss."

Buddy whimpered for attention. The desperate sound seemed to pull Sam from his reverie, and he stood and squared his bony shoulders. Slow, thoughtful steps took him to his workbench, where he continued his project. He held the lid in progress in front of him, checking what he'd done as he continued his conversation with Annie. He never forgot anything. Sometimes, though, he would think a while before responding. Now he said, "Sometimes we wonder why God does what He does, but we have to trust His plan. He created us. In God's eyes, we are masterpieces."

He threw her a smile and she breathed in relief. "He loves us so much, and even though we may not understand why things happen, He does. And there's a reason behind every decision He makes."

Sam focused on his work, but Annie couldn't get Patricia and Elaine out of her mind. She gave a quick shake of her head to clear it. "Sam, when you lost Esther, didn't you miss her terribly?" The tension in her hands went away and she dropped them to her sides.

Sam chuckled. Annie loved his laugh. The timbre of his voice was joyful. "Little one, we can't expect to stay on this earth forever. My father used to tell me that the real secret to happiness isn't what you give or receive; it's what you share. And what I shared with Esther was the best blessing God ever could have given me, not to mention eternity in heaven together. What better gift could I have? Patience isn't always easy, but when we let God guide our lives, we're on the path to salvation."

She gave an accepting nod. "But you must miss her. I know I do. Because she always made us sponge cakes."

After a big grin, he went back to carving away at the wood. "And now you make them for me. She'd be pleased. Not a minute goes by when I don't think of her. But God will let me be with her again, and next time will be even better than our earth days. Besides, my work here isn't finished. Think of all the folks who order these chests for loved ones. You know what they say about it being better to give others a piece of your heart than a piece of your mind."

Annie giggled.

"It's what's inside of us that really makes us special."

Annie marveled at his faith. She knew God would take care of her, too, but wondered if her belief would ever be as strong as Sam's. Maybe when you got old, your faith got stronger. By that time you'd have a lot of opportunities to think about things.

"Annie, God's plan is bigger than anything we can imagine." His eyes sparkled as he eyed her. "Of course we'll have to wait to get to heaven to see what it is."

She leaned forward and put a confident hand on her hip. "You know what I think?" Before he could answer, she went on in an excited voice. "I agree with you. God puts us here to do a job."

Sam pressed his lips together and nodded in agreement.

"After we finish it, He pulls us into heaven."

Buddy rolled onto his back. Annie knew him so well; he wanted his tummy rubbed. Annie bent to gently move her hand over the sensitive area while Buddy moaned in delight. But Annie's mind stayed on their conversation.

"Why do you think God put you here, Annie?"

She let out a happy sigh. "That's easy. To take care of you."

Sam's lips lifted into a wide grin. "I don't doubt that for a minute. I'm not sure what I'd do without you three girls. Rebecca brings me wildflowers. Rachel listens to my horse-and-buggy stories over and over, and you . . . how would I survive without your sponge cakes?"

Annie lifted a shoulder. "You would go hungry."

They laughed.

"I'm not sure, but I suspect Esther would be impressed. You're turning into quite the cook."

Annie's voice lifted in excitement. "Really?"

Sam gave a firm nod and grinned. "Back to Elaine. She specifically requested an image to depict the future of her only daughter and husband-to-be."

Annie thought a moment and pressed her lips together. At the same time, she tapped her foot against the barn's concrete floor. Buddy nudged Annie's ankle with a long, red, hairy leg.

Automatically, Annie bent to run an obedient hand over the canine's back. "She's leaving it to your imagination?"

He nodded. A huge grin followed. "This is the part of the job I love the most. It's like choosing a book cover. But I admit I've been undecided. And there's not much time to make up my mind. So . . . I decided the future of the new couple would be a flower garden."

He moved to the other side of the bench and faced her. For a moment, white flecks danced in his wise eyes. "Let me explain." He paused to rub some particle board off his work and evaluate what was in front of him. "In a flower garden are many varieties of plants. Lovely petals. You might see a bright pink tulip alongside a plant without any bloom at all. Some are tall; some short. Perennials and annuals. When one dies, another appears. And if you allow your imagination to wander a bit, you'll see it's the same with life. There are beautiful moments and painful ones."

She lifted her chin. "Like birth and death."

"But in life everything's thrown in together. Life can toss difficult situations at you, but because God takes care of us, we know those moments will go away and we'll see the sunshine again."

"I guess you're right. Kind of like rain. You can't do much, but then when the sun comes out, you forget about the dreariness."

He nodded. "And marriage is sort of like that, too."

She waited for him to continue. He stood and meandered to the door and she walked beside him. "There might be a perfect-looking daisy. In life, there might be a day when everything goes the way you pray for it to." He paused to rub the back of his neck. "On the other hand, there are times when obstacles hit you from every direction. That's where faith comes in."

As Annie watched him, she considered his wisdom. In the English world, there were surely doctors and lawyers who would envy Old Sam's ability to reason. She didn't know them personally, but there was one thing she was sure of: No one could figure things out like Sam. He knew the answers to everything. Annie yearned to talk to him about her feelings for Levi. If it was wrong to wish she could be with someone who wasn't Amish. If she was a sinner for even daring to imagine spending every moment with a person who no longer practiced her faith.

But she considered what Sam had said. If Annie believed as she had been taught, wouldn't God figure out a way for her to be with her best friend? As Annie tried to make sense of reality, a light breeze slipped in through the open door and scattered sawdust particles everywhere. To the side, Sam's horse, Ginger, whinnied for attention. She stuck her head out of her stall.

Annie's thoughts drifted to Levi and the realization that she might as well stop thinking about him. Her pulse slowed to a disappointing pace. Would Levi ever join the Amish church? He already knew the Pennsylvania Dutch language.

But her own community, the very body of people who had raised her to forgive, had shunned his father. As a result, their families were divided.

A future with Levi Miller would be a road that would never be built. But was she really sure about that? Sam's words about faith stuck in her mind.

"What are you thinking, young one?"

Pulled from her reverie, Annie sighed in relief. Sam always seemed to read her thoughts. "It's about Levi."

His lips curved into an amused line. The deep green of his eyes lightened a shade. "I figured." The words were followed by a quick wink.

She pressed her fingers to her chin and spoke in her most adult tone. "Sam, what if you wanted to be with a person who went to a different church?"

"Marry?"

She thought a moment. "Maybe."

A long silence passed as he carved. Moments later, he put his knife aside on the lid. "Let's take a ride to your house. We can talk on the way. I've been meaning to discuss church stuff with your father."

She smiled in relief. Old Sam was going to answer her questions. Soon she wouldn't have to worry about what to do or think about Levi anymore. Sam would know. He gave the best advice. Ever.

When they stepped outside of the barn, she blinked as the bright sun hit her face. The large orange ball came out from behind a white fluffy cloud.

In the buggy, Annie stretched her legs and breathed in happiness. She loved rides with Sam. As they moved forward, Ginger yanked on the reins. The old Standardbred knew the route by heart. Sam ran a thoughtful finger through his long gray beard and spoke in a serious tone. "I'm still thinking about your question about the Miller boy. And I guess the answer is really up to you."

"But . . ."

Sam paused. "Let me ask you this: How important are your beliefs to you?"

It didn't take Annie long to answer. "I've never really given them much thought, but really, they're everything." She felt obligated to clarify why she'd said that. "I mean, when I think about it, my faith is the way I live, how I think; I'm pretty sure my decisions come from what I believe." Annie realized, though, that at her age, she hadn't yet made any big choices. The thought of being with Levi was by far the most complicated issue she'd confronted.

"Hmm."

Annie adjusted herself in her seat, smoothing the soft blanket beneath her, which Esther had crocheted. She was sure Sam would never take it off the hard wooden bench.

Annie enjoyed the familiar view before her. Cows grazing. Baby goats. To her far right was her own backyard. From a distance, she glimpsed the clothes on Mamma's line, moving up and down with the breeze. A mouthwatering aroma floated through the air, making her stomach grumble. She was pretty sure the delicious-smelling scent was shepherd's pie. Mamma baked it on Wednesday afternoons and everyone in town knew it was the best. Maybe one day Annie would learn how to make it herself, for when she had her own home and family.

"I think you can come up with your own answer."

Annie contemplated his words. "How on earth can I do that?"

"It's really simpler than you're making it out to be. Just ask yourself this: Let's say there's the Amish church. At the same time, there's a man you like. If you could only choose one, which would it be?"

Annie frowned at the poignant question.

"I don't know. What if both are equally important?"

"You can only pick one."

She thought a moment. She wasn't sure. "How on earth can I decide?"

A stunned look crossed Sam's face. Long moments passed as she tried to interpret his expression.

"What would you have done if Esther had gone to a different church?"

A long silence ensued as tears filled his eyes. He seemed to swallow a large knot in his throat. His voice was emotional, his words coming out barely in a whisper. "It's impossible to say."

She studied his serious expression.

"You see, if Esther hadn't been Amish, I wouldn't have courted her."

Annie let the words sink in before she countered, "But what if she had left the faith and you became reacquainted with her? Like Levi and me? What would you have done?"

Later that day, Annie's heart pumped with uncertainty as she considered that conversation with Sam. She and her sister were hanging fresh noodles on the clothesline they'd set up in the kitchen.

"It was a nice wedding, *jah*?"

Elizabeth's soft voice broke the silence. At the end of the dark-stained oak table, Annie darted a curious glance at her sister as she drained water. The sisters' eyes met, and Annie realized her older, married sibling awaited a response.

"Sorry," Annie apologized. "I was thinking about Old Sam and the hope chest he's working on." She gave a quick, agreeable nod. "The wedding was wonderful." She drew in a deep, satisfied breath and locked excited gazes with Lizzie.

The tantalizing aroma of Mamma's pork roast and cabbage baking in the oven floated through the air.

"Jeremiah and Katie looked so happy. The weather couldn't have been more perfect. And the food . . . oh!"

Elizabeth agreed.

Annie began hanging noodle strips on the wall-to-wall line. "They'll make good parents."

"And I hear Katie makes a tasty raspberry cobbler. They're living on the outskirts of town with her folks while they help them get situated in the *dawdy* house," Lizzie said, referring to the grandparents' house.

Then Lizzie eyed Annie with a curious, raised brow. "At the wedding . . . did you get a chance to chat with Rebecca Conrad?"

Annie shook her head.

Lizzie sighed. "She and William seem happy, too. Rebecca and I caught up. They've been in their place a few months now. It's finished enough to live in, but they're still painting and working on the inside."

"Really?"

Lizzie responded with an immediate nod. "William's doing well with his cabinet shop and Rebecca helps with the bookwork and does her own projects."

Annie looked at her to continue.

"She started her own dried floral business. She's in to wreaths and such."

Annie considered the news. "That doesn't surprise me. Now that you mention it, I remember when she used to make a big thing about gardening. She loved it. And her yard was always a showpiece."

"I remember when out-of-towners drove by her folks' house to catch a look at the beautiful flower garden in front."

Annie smiled a little. "I had no idea she'd made her hobby into a livelihood. *Gut* for her!"

"I guess she decided to do it when she spent the summer away, helping William's dad. She did a lot of thinking and praying and . . ." Lizzie raised her palms to the sky. "She made the decision. The girl even grows her own plants for the wreaths."

Annie had always been fond of Rebecca. Her

sister's good friend was so kind, and there was something about her generosity that made you want to be around her.

Annie pressed her lips together in uncertainty at the thought of Rebecca following her heart. No doubt Mrs. Conrad would excel at whatever she pursued. Rebecca was . . . perfection. Annie had always envied the way she did everything right.

But it hadn't always been easy for Rebecca or her family. Not that long ago, Rebecca had started the community buzzing when she traveled to Indiana to help William's shunned father. In fact, Annie recalled hearing rumors about Rebecca and William leaving the community to join his folks. But gossip had been just that. It was ridiculous. William and Rebecca had come back, just as they'd promised, and joined the church.

Annie knew what it was like to have a dream. She yearned for a large family. Lots of daughters. She longed to teach them to make light, tasty sponge cakes. And to quilt. And to live at Pebble Creek.

She wanted a cat. Like the one she and Levi had shared. A nice, new house near her parents. But the image in her mind missed one piece: a man. So far, she hadn't even courted. To her knowledge, no eligible bachelor within ten miles of town was interested in her. And vice versa.

During the long silence that ensued between the sisters, she allowed her hopeful thoughts to drift to the many bags of noodles they would auction to raise money for the new school desks and books. The school where Annie now taught.

This past summer, Annie had sold produce

roadside in hopes of making extra cash. Because of the special project for the children, she was willing to sacrifice having personal money. Hopefully, she'd have enough left over to buy material for a new dress this winter. And, with good fortune, the weather would be nice, so there'd be a great turnout.

"I was surprised Levi Miller was there."

The unexpected comment prompted Annie to drop a piece of dough. While she bent to retrieve it, her pulse quickened, but she certainly tried not to show it. It would fuel the fire around her about staying away from her "English" friend. Thinking of a way to change the subject, she continued cutting dough and hanging the strands on the line.

Finally, she forced a disinterested tone. The last thing she wanted was for anyone to know she hadn't thought of anything but Levi since the wedding. "Why?" she finally got out. "He's Jeremiah's first cousin."

"Of course he is. But his dad was shunned. I just figured we'd never see them again. I had written him off."

Pretending she didn't care, Annie kept her tone distant. "I'm glad he came. Besides, Levi was never shunned, only his father." Annie couldn't stop the words that followed. "And I never did think what happened to him was fair."

"Annie!"

Lizzie's raised voice prompted Annie to drop another string of pasta. "See what you did, Lizzie? Now I've wasted this good piece," she harrumphed.

"Sorry. Annie . . ." Elizabeth lowered her voice to a more confidential tone. "You know how important it is to follow the rules. And as far as Levi . . . I couldn't help but notice the two of you talking. Or the way you looked at each other. Something told me you'd be wanting him to come."

Annie pressed her lips together and remembered his warm smile when they had become reacquainted. She didn't respond to Lizzie's observation.

"He's turned into such a handsome man." Lizzie rolled her eyes and added, "It's no secret you two used to be inseparable. Don't think I've forgotten how you followed him around when we were children."

Annie crossed defensive arms across her chest and lifted her chin. "I did *not* follow him around." She paused. "He's older than me and I always sort of looked up to him."

"And I understand why. He did watch out for you. As I recall, he even covered for you once when you were late getting to school."

They giggled.

Lizzie continued. "He was big for his age. He and William Conrad."

Annie smiled a little. "I remember watching them carry bales of hay from the pasture and into the barn."

Lizzie grinned. "Couldn't count on both my hands the number of times you weren't on time for dinner 'cause you and Levi were out doing something." Lizzie paused. "Of course you always had a tendency to run behind."

Annie couldn't argue with that. She'd been scolded more times than she wanted to remember for tardiness. But she was older now. She tried to do better.

Her mind was flooded with memories of her childhood best friend. The recollections prompted her heart to warm. But the last thing Annie wanted to talk about was Levi. Why wouldn't she be fond of him? At the same time, she wished she didn't want to spend time with him. After all, he was English. And her life would be empty when he returned to his world.

"That was a long time ago, Lizzie. We were kids. Now things are different. But I was glad to see him. And we caught up a bit." She gave a casual shrug of her shoulders, as if she hadn't thought of him since. She'd been cheated out of ten years of a great friendship because of his dad's actions and her church's response.

Annie was fully aware of how strict the rules were. But the shunning hadn't benefited John Miller. Or his family. Or the Amish faith. God was all about forgiveness. And no one was perfect. Shouldn't they have talked it out and welcomed him back with open arms? Shouldn't there have been another way to chastise Levi's dad without shunning him? It seemed so drastic.

"Annie?" Her sister grinned in amusement.

"What?"

"I caught you looking over at him. And," she added, "I saw him staring at you."

Annie stopped what she was doing. "He was?" Suddenly, the blood rushed to Annie's face in embarrassment. Lizzie had gotten the best of her. Annie knew better than to set her sights on Levi.

And she wouldn't. Besides, Lizzie was nosy. Annie wished she hadn't shown any interest. Now it was time to nix any curiosity Lizzie had about Levi.

"You want to know something?"

Annie waited.

"Talk is that David Stutzman wants to court you."

Annie's brows drew together in a frown. "Now where'd you hear that?"

"At the singing last week."

Annie considered this development. She liked David very much. She didn't know him well, but he was nice. His parents were well-respected farmers who owned a lot of cattle and specialized in dairy. David was two years older than her. He was . . . jovial.

"Annie, the family's honest and hardworking. There's no better man in town than his father. And word has it that David's just like him."

Annie gave a dismissive shrug. "He seems shy."

Lizzie raised her voice. "Annie, he's not. Oh . . ." She stopped herself.

"What were you going to say?"

Lizzie's voice was edged with uncertainty. "Maybe he's just bashful around you."

"What's that supposed to mean?"

"It's just that . . . sometimes . . ." She took a decisive breath and met Annie's defensive gaze. "I imagine boys might be a little intimidated by your directness. I mean, maybe you shouldn't say so much? Other girls aren't quite so . . . verbal. I know you don't mean to scare boys off."

Annie squared her shoulders and took in her sister's uncertain expression. "Do you know how ridiculous that sounds? Why on earth would I hide what I'm feeling? I don't want to be anything other than straight to the point. Still, I don't know how I could scare anyone off." She shook her head in dismay. "And if a man's afraid of me 'cause I speak my mind, maybe he's not enough for me."

Lizzie's eyes doubled in size.

"I'm serious. I don't know what my future holds, but I am sure of this: whoever spends his life with me will have to take me the way I am. And if I don't marry?" She lifted her palms to the ceiling. "So be it. I want someone who likes me for me. Nothing less."

Chapter Five

The next day, the sun moved across the sky and hid behind a large puffy cloud. Levi blinked as it quickly reappeared. He sensed Annie was coming. They hadn't made plans, yet he was sure she would join him here. He smiled a little when he glimpsed her making her way to the edge of Pebble Creek.

Levi's pulse picked up speed as he thought of her large, hopeful eyes that were the most extraordinary shade of blue. Their depth was so beautiful, they were almost magical. Flecks of a much lighter, gentler hue danced on her pupils when she looked at him.

He silently chastised himself, then wondered why. *What I'm feeling surely can't be unusual for a man to feel toward a woman. Even if I were still Amish, I don't know what could stop my heart from racing. But why am I compelled to see her again? I know better. I'm fully aware I'm approaching a seemingly impossible situation. When we were young nothing could have separated us.*

But something had—the shunning—and that act, which neither of them had been involved in, had formed an invisible wall between them. Forever. At the same time, when he was with Annie, he felt so . . . important. She listened to everything he said. Nothing he broached wasn't worth talking about. For some reason, when he was with Annie, he was *home.*

He tapped the toe of his shoe against the hard earth to a nervous beat, trying to make sense of what drew him to her. What he did know with clear certainty was that when he was with Annie, his heart pumped a little harder than usual. And his level of happiness was uncharted territory.

"Hello." Her voice was breathless and soft. When her lips lifted into a generous smile, he grinned back, taking the basket she handed him. "I brought some snacks."

"How did you know I'd be here?"

When she giggled, her cheeks deepened in color. "I just knew. Because this is your favorite place in the world. And I'm glad we have more time together. To catch up," she added. "What's funny is . . ." She caught her breath. "In a way, I feel like we're still kids." She pulled in a deep, decisive breath. "You're the same old Levi I chummed around with." She gestured with her hands. "When we were little, you dreamed about building a home here. You still think about it?"

He bit his lip in frustration. He knew better than to become too much at ease with Annie. Here, at his favorite spot in the world. Just because they were at Pebble Creek, the place they'd spent afternoons together sharing those dreams, didn't mean they could just pick up where they'd left off. Circumstances had changed. Though their friendship was as strong as ever, they were different. Her lifestyle was miles away from his.

She frowned. "What's wrong? You want to talk about it?"

As they walked uphill along the creek, Levi gave careful consideration to her question. His thoughts should be no surprise to her. After all, she knew the rules like the back of her hand. And she knew him. Even after years of separation. As he thought of a response, gentle gurgling sounds from the flowing water cascading over the pebblelike rocks echoed throughout the mesmerizing parcel of land. Above, the sun and the clouds didn't budge. There was no breeze. Utter stillness. It was as if nature was taking a break.

Salty tears stung his eyes. He blinked. "I love this land." He gazed at the creek. "The very water that separates this vacant spot from your home."

She cleared her throat. "Levi, I wish you'd come back to live here."

As soon as she made her confession, he could tell she regretted saying it. But her directness was what he liked about her. One of the things, anyway.

He smiled, but didn't respond. "I've always respected your honesty. I never have to guess where you're coming from."

"I get that all the time; that I should be more like my older sister."

He frowned. "That's nonsense. Why would you want to be like her?"

"To please Mamma. I don't want to disappoint her. Or Lizzie." A laugh escaped her. "I think they're afraid of me being a spinster."

"A spinster? I doubt you'll have to worry about that. I'm sure if the boys are shy around you it's because you're so pretty."

Her cheeks reddened. "Really?"

"Surely that doesn't surprise you. And you *are* a bit more direct than other Amish girls your age, but you know what?"

She looked at him, waiting for him to continue.

"That's what makes you special."

"Jah?"

He gave a slow but sure nod, taking in the happy light that danced in her eyes. As they continued walking in silence, he thought of something for the first time. Like her, he was straightforward. Both of them were open books really. Maybe that was why they got along so well. And he didn't regret for a moment what he'd just said. He wanted to make sure Annie knew just how he felt. That she was unique. Until now, he hadn't realized just how much he'd missed this special friendship. Accepting how important she was, he eyed her from his peripheral vision, his lips parted. Right here at his fingertips was everything he could ever dream of having. His heart skipped a beat. All of it had been taken away by one single act.

At the top of the hill, they stopped and sat down on the stones that had been there for over ten years. With one careful motion, Levi set the basket between them, trying to shrug off what had become obvious to him. The reality was that everything was the same, yet everything was different.

Directing his attention to the beautiful girl beside him, he focused on the contents of her small wicker basket. "Hmm. I wonder what's in it."

She grinned. "It's a surprise. But I'll give you a hint. It's your favorite snack. At least, it used to be." She opened the lid and pulled out two sponge cakes wrapped in plastic. She handed him a napkin with one of the treats and retrieved the other cake and napkin for herself.

"You're the best cook around, I'm sure."

She laughed. "You're just being nice."

"No; I mean it. Maybe I've just forgotten how good these taste. In fact, if my memory's up to par, the last one I ate was with you, right here on our spot by Pebble Creek."

They talked while they ate. "If you'll recall, you're the one who came up with the name."

"Pebble Creek?"

She lifted her chin. While she chewed, he took in the creaminess of her skin, firmly reminding himself that any romantic interest in her was strictly forbidden from her side yet, to his dismay, it existed on his part. That silent admission made him stiffen. What was wrong with him?

"I remember now. About Pebble Creek. We were walking and laughing, like today. Throwing rocks into the water and watching it splatter." She inhaled, as if taking a break. "Anyway, we decided no matter what the name of the creek really was, to us it would always be Pebble Creek."

He snapped his fingers. "Yup."

"I don't know where all the pebbles came from. But today . . ." She waved a hand toward the narrow, shallow body of water. "The pebbles remind me that this must be the most beautiful creek in the world. And the most peaceful."

"I've missed you, Annie."

"I've missed you, too. Levi, please promise me you'll never leave." Before he could reply, she added, "Please."

He laughed. Not because of what she was asking but because of the direct, honest way in which she said it. And he believed that was what truly made her different from any other girl he had ever met.

She pleaded. "Stay. Levi, you can still build a house right here." She dropped her hand to her side. "You love this place. Nothing's stopping you."

Levi frowned. The last thing he wanted was to disappoint his one true friend. But what she was asking . . . he couldn't ignore it. He had to admit to himself and explain to her that he could never move back because of the hard feelings he still had. What she'd asked deserved an answer. "Annie, when we were young, things were simple."

"They still are. Levi, you don't have some terrible illness. Neither do I. When you put things into perspective, the world's at our doorstep. Will we face obstacles?" Before he could respond, she answered her own question. "Of course. But we can create our own outcomes. Don't you agree?"

He laughed at her logic. "You might have a point. About the shunning . . . you're right, Annie. It wasn't life threatening. And my family came out of it just fine. But at the time, and for a long time after it happened, it was so painful . . . I mean, it changed our family forever. I could never pretend it didn't happen. Besides, my lifestyle . . ."

She shook her head in protest. "Levi, I don't care. We'll figure something out. I know we can. I'll help you. You know what they say about there being a way if there's a will?" She lowered the timbre of her voice to a heart-felt plea. Before he could answer, she jumped in again. "You're my best friend. Forever." She quickly added, "Besides Old Sam."

Her admission pulled at his heartstrings. He squared his shoulders and straightened his back. He couldn't let emotions get the better of him. No matter how much Annie wanted him to stay, he couldn't. He forced a smile. "How's Sam doing? Does he still make those hope chests?"

She offered a quick nod. "And I make him sponge cakes." She rolled her eyes. "I can't let him starve, Levi."

A grin tugged his lips as he contemplated Old Sam and the three who looked after him. Since Levi's return, he'd heard all about Esther's death and how Annie, Rachel, and Rebecca made sure he was well taken care of.

"Sam has it pretty good, Annie."

"You think?"

"You bake for him and Rachel listens to his stories. Of course, Rebecca's married now . . ."

"Oh, but she still takes him flowers."

He threw her an amused smile. "You see what I mean? Sam must be the envy of every guy in town."

"Speaking of Rebecca, it seems she and William are happy."

"I'm glad."

"William's father was really sick for a while; William went to Indiana to help with his cabinet business."

Levi offered a nod. "I know bits and pieces of the story from talking with William at the wedding. That he even left the Amish community for a while."

Levi couldn't imagine Annie's strict Amish parents allowing her that opportunity. Not even during *Rumspringa.*

Annie nodded. "Lizzie and I were talking about it yesterday. Rebecca's parents' approval didn't come easy. The bishop finally offered his blessing under the condition that she accomplish certain goals while she was away. And in the end . . ." Annie threw her hands to the sky and shrugged. "It actually proved to be a good thing. For both of them."

Levi laughed. He could hardly imagine that, but he knew it was true from his conversation with William.

"William was at odds with his dad because he moved out-of-state to marry outside the faith."

Levi let out a low whistle.

Annie gave a quick nod. "It was a shock to everyone. And then Daniel left William behind . . ."

Levi shook his head before offering a wry smile. "It couldn't have been all bad, though. His auntie Sarah's the best. Still, I imagine William's relationship with Daniel was pretty rocky after that."

For long moments, Levi considered the shunning and the big move his family had made to an English lifestyle. "At least my dad took me with him. You're right when you said that things could always be worse. Can you imagine life without your own father?"

Annie gave a firm shake of her head. A long, comfortable silence passed while they leaned back on their elbows. In front of them, cascades of water rolled over the path of big pebbles, eventually falling into the creek. The scene was so serene, beautiful, and this time with Annie was precious. He never wanted it to end.

Years ago, moments like this had been plentiful. His stomach tied in knots when he thought of leaving.

Annie's voice was edged with a combination of persistence and desperation. "Levi, I wish there was some way your daddy could reconcile with the Amish." She put up a defensive hand. "I know what you're going to say. That I'm the eternal optimist. That I always want a happy ending. But, Levi, I keep telling you, we make our own endings. Many times it's within our power to make changes to our paths. Don't you think?"

Levi gave a slow, sad shake of his head. "Annie, too many years have gone by and too much has happened. And I'm not sure that's a bad thing. To be honest, I can't imagine my dad wanting to be Amish again. And in his demanding work, I don't know how he'd make it without owning and driving a truck. Not to mention electricity."

"Old Sam has his own business and he does fine without it."

When the sun moved across the sky, the temperature dropped a notch. Levi knew the day would soon be over and this might be his last time with Annie. The thought prompted an ache in his chest.

Her voice broke his reverie. "Let's get back to you. Tell me about your house. What you do these days."

He offered a casual shrug. "What d'you want to know?"

"Details." Her demand was followed by a shy grin.

"We live in the country. Our place is bricked in front; it's two stories, with four bedrooms. My room's upstairs; the folks sleep on the ground level." He hesitated. "According to Mom, the kitchen is a cook's dream."

Annie pressed her hands together and let out a wistful sigh. "Why? Is it huge?"

"Yup, but the way it's designed is unique. Mom helped Dad and me draw up the plans." He paused. "In the middle of the kitchen is what we call an island." Before she could get in a question, he went on, "With a stove and a chopping block. And what's really cool is that stainless-steel pots and pans hang from the ceiling. The roof's high, but it dips in that particular spot. I guess you could say it's space friendly."

"What about the walls?"

"Cream-colored; the ceiling is a light shade of turquoise."

"Cabinets?"

"Cherry. With matching dining room table and chairs."

"Sounds beautiful."

"I should have thought to take pictures on my cell phone. So you could see for yourself."

Annie's voice softened with disappointment. "So really, you did get that new house you always dreamed of."

Levi hesitated, then said, "No. It's not at Pebble Creek." He thought of the future. "I still dream of building here for my own family." A long uncomfortable silence ensued as he considered his own words. When he glanced at her, Annie's expression was unreadable. He hoped his own thoughts were as well.

What he'd said was true. Yeah, he wanted a family. He looked forward to designing a house with his dad, a place for him, his wife, and kids.

He thought of Annie. She, too, would marry someday. The Amish usually wed young, so he was certain it would most likely happen in the next few years. A hard, uncomfortable lump formed in his throat that he tried to swallow. To his dismay, it remained.

They had easily picked up where they'd left off. As if they'd never been separated. But . . . he regarded her from the corner of his eye. As he studied her, his heart picked up to a fast, unsteady beat. He chastised himself, but he was a guy. And during their years apart, Annie had turned into an extremely beautiful woman. He couldn't deny what was right in front of him, and there was no way to ignore it.

There was nothing ostentatious about Annie; there didn't have to be. Her loveliness was simple, quiet, subtle. Of course Amish girls didn't wear makeup. Obviously she wasn't obsessed with fashion. Simplicity was one of her most attractive traits. Along with her high cheekbones. And her large blue eyes with long dark lashes. And her soft, silky-looking skin. The only thing he would change about her was her hairstyle; he'd love to see her blond strands loose. He wondered how long they were. If there were natural highlights.

He stopped himself. Thinking of Annie as anything other than a friend was foolish. He couldn't marry her. They lived two different lives, and he was sure she planned to join the Amish church. Though she hadn't joined yet . . . Maybe he could convince her to become English.

Levi noticed her watching him. If she could read his mind, his cheeks would be as red as the bright shade on the American flag. Good thing she couldn't.

"How about the yard? Is it large? Fenced? Do you own cattle? Horses?" As she leaned forward, impatience edged her voice. "Come on! You can't leave me hanging!"

He shifted to a more comfortable position. His feelings for her were still strong, but she had changed. And so had he. They were no longer carefree children. They were adults. *Has she thought of marrying someone in the Amish community?* That question nagged at him.

He tried to push it out of his mind by addressing her questions. "We have a car. Cattle?" He shook his head. "However, we do have hens. To be honest, the transition from Amish to English wasn't all that difficult. If only restarting Dad's business had been as easy."

"I imagine. But he's such a talented builder. There was never a doubt in my mind that he would succeed. But what he had to go through . . . I mean all of you," she corrected herself. "Over the years, I've always kept you in my prayers."

After that admission he gently caressed her hand and squeezed it. But touching her like this was crossing the line. She allowed it. There was something between them . . . he knew it and guessed she did, too. Yet he wasn't sure what the strong, unchartered emotion was. "Thank you, Annie. That means a lot." He paused. "I kept you and your family in mine, too."

"Yeah?"

"Yup."

"What did you pray?"

His lips curved into a mischievous grin when their eyes locked. The hazy flecks in hers lulled him in to another world. Mesmerized, he stared into her deep Mediterranean blue eyes and lost his train of thought. The gorgeous color captivated him even more than usual as the sun lightened the hue to the most mesmerizing shade he'd ever seen. When she raised her chin a notch, he suddenly realized she was waiting for an answer, so he quickly looked away to think more clearly.

"I prayed for God to protect you." He grinned, adding, "And for you not to get into trouble for your directness."

They shared a laugh.

She lowered her voice. "Sometimes I think I must disappoint my parents."

"Why?"

"'Cause they always talk about how Elizabeth is so perfect." Annie sighed and added, "She is."

"You know what I really like about you?"

She shook her head.

"That you're independent."

Excitement entered her voice. *"Jah?"*

He nodded.

"But I wish I were more like Elizabeth and the other Amish girls my age. They don't question things the way I do. Lizzie is perfectly happy doing what she's expected to do."

He cocked his head. "Is that a good thing?"

"I think so." She did a helpless roll of her eyes. "The rules don't leave much room for questions. Everything is pretty cut and dried. But sometimes I don't know if I can live up to everyone's expectations."

Her honest admission surprised him. "Annie, don't try so hard."

"But I have to, Levi. I can't ignore it 'cause it won't be long before I have to decide whether to join the church. But when I think of the strict standard everyone expects, sometimes I wonder . . ."

"What?"

"If I measure up."

He smiled with understanding. "But you were raised that way."

"That doesn't mean I've made everyone happy. It seems like Mamma is always waiting on me to go somewhere. I'm not even a good cook. Except for sponge cakes."

His lips curved with amusement. "You always ran a little late when I came by to walk you to school. But in the scheme of things, that's minor."

"I've tried to be more prompt. And I'm doing my best to become a better cook."

He cleared his throat. "There's something I'd like to do before I head back home." He paused to clear his throat. "Remember that trip to Six Flags I promised you years ago?"

That night, in slow, uncertain motions, Levi folded a pair of socks and packed them into his small suitcase. He glanced around the four corners of his cousin's bedroom and pressed his lips together in deep thought. His time here was ending. It was hard to believe the wedding had been only four days ago. Standing, he pressed his finger against his chin and glanced out of the window.

As he took in the view in front of him, vivid memories raced through his mind. His life used to be simple, like this. He stepped closer to the window and glimpsed visions of yesterday. The large red barn where he'd helped stack bales of hay. Cattle. Chickens running through the yard. Tall oak trees that shaded the house in the summertime. He swallowed an emotional knot and for the first time realized that not everything here was bad. In fact, there were certain parts of this place he wished he could put in his travel bag and take with him. Like Annie.

That thought stopped him. He shook his head and silently scolded himself for allowing his mind to go there again. He had suffered every bit as much as his dad. In the process of leaving town, he'd lost the person most dear to him: Annie. He'd taken for granted she would always be there for him. And now that he'd found her again, he didn't want to let her go.

Sounds of dishes clinking floated up the stairs. His aunt kept such a clean kitchen; dirty plates didn't stay in the sink long. He looked around himself; there wasn't a trace of dust. Of course there wasn't much to dust around in this austere room.

He looked down at his hand, lingering on the suitcase handle as he revisited yesterday's conversation.

There was more that troubled him than leaving Annie. Not sure what it was, he thought of all they had discussed.

"Please don't go."

He closed his eyes. Her heartfelt words had etched themselves into his heart. But he'd get over this. He had to. The moment he left, he could never look back.

That same evening, Annie's mind also was on her conversation with Levi. Her chest ached at the thought of never seeing him again.

Her mother's voice startled her. "Annie? Did you hear what I said?" Mamma motioned to a kitchen chair and continued churning.

Annie took the seat and faced her role model. The enticing smell of creamy homemade butter filled Annie's nostrils. Mamma was about the only person around who still made her own. Everyone else bought it. But Mamma loved doing it. And she took pride in the end result. And that was fine with Annie. Even though she wasn't fond of cattle, at least something good came from them.

"You want to talk about him?"

Annie was quick to detect concern in her mother's soft voice. "What?"

Her mother sighed and continued her task. "Levi Miller." Her voice softened to an understanding tone.

Annie looked down at the wood floor. When she lifted her eyes, she met her mother's inquisitive gaze.

"There's really not much to say, Mamma. The

shunning forced Levi's family to move away and start all over." She exhaled and raised her voice. "There's nothing that can ever change that." She lifted her shoulders. "Why did something so devastating have to happen? I still don't understand."

The expression in her mother's eyes was a combination of uncertainty and disappointment. "Like it or not, in any faith, there are standards, and if a person chooses not to follow them, he must be prepared for discipline."

"I know; I just wish things could be different. Obviously the Millers aren't coming back to our church, but why not mend the fence? Nothing good came out of what happened." She threw her hands in the air. "Life is too short."

"Annie, there have been others in the community who were shunned but chose to stay here. I can't help it that Levi's father didn't want to do that." She paused to push out a deep breath. "I know how you don't like drama. That you want everybody happy. But, honey, life isn't perfect. You know that. Even you are always saying that this isn't a perfect world."

Annie waited for her mother to continue.

"We can't fight every battle and win. There are some things you just have to accept." Mamma's lips lifted into a gentle smile.

"I'm aware you like Levi. Your friendship with the boy is beautiful. When you went to school together, why, you never stopped talking about him. And I'm not denying what a fine child he was. I'll never forget how hard he worked, baling hay for your uncle. Never once heard him complain about the heat. Your dad and I thought . . ." She stopped.

Annie leaned closer so her shoes touched the tall, heavy butter churn. She cocked her head in curiosity. "What did you and dad think?"

With a careless shrug of her shoulders, Mamma lifted a finger to push back a lone black hair that had escaped her covering. "We thought he would make a good husband for you." Before Annie could respond, her mother went on. "Of course . . . that was years ago. And there are other nice young men, honey. Did you notice how David Stutzman made it a point to talk to you after the wedding dinner?" She sweetened her voice. "I think he likes you, Annie."

Annie frowned.

Mamma rested a firm hand on her hip. "What's wrong with the Stutzman boy? Now, don't you go writing him off. He's hardworking; he'd make a good husband." Mamma used her most defensive tone.

"Mamma, not tonight." Annie waved a hand. "I don't want to hear any more about him. He's nice and all, but I can't imagine spending the rest of my life with someone so . . ."

Her mother lifted a disappointed brow. "So what?"

Annie giggled. "Boring."

"Annie, what do you think marriage is?" To Annie's chagrin, Mamma's tone sharpened.

Annie shrugged.

"Well, I'll tell you. It's supporting each other. Annie, he's from a good, honest family. Don't forget that love should be based on respect more than emotion. Of course it's wonderful to have both. But as you get older, you'll see that lending a helping hand or taking care of children speaks true love. What's more important than that?"

Annie contemplated the question. "Nothing. Levi's a hard worker." Tired of defending her opinion, she forced a reassuring smile to her face and threw an affectionate arm around the person she loved most in the world. "*Don't worry.* If I marry, he'll be Amish."

She started up the stairs. When she turned, she was quick to note concern lines around her mother's eyes. "Mamma, what have I done to make you doubt me?"

There was no response.

Annie took another step before turning back to glance at her mother again. "Mamma, if God wants me to marry, He'll give me a husband."

Mamma's expression finally relaxed. She smiled a little and turned back to her work. "He will. And whoever it is will have to hold his own around you."

Chapter Six

Two days later Annie was almost jumping with excitement as they arrived at Six Flags. The decade-old dream of hers and Levi's was about to come true.

With a quick motion, Levi flipped off the car's heater and the quiet sound of air flowing from the vents ceased. As he made his way down aisle after aisle, Annie took in the license plates from different states. Her jaw dropped in surprise. "Apparently we're not the only ones who came a long way."

"Obviously not."

Annie pointed to an open space and Levi carefully made his way in between the two solid lines, pushing out an exaggerated sigh of relief. He darted her a satisfied glance before checking the rearview mirror.

"Good thing I have a small car. I was starting to wonder if we would see more than this lot today. By the looks of it, everyone in America came here." He turned off the ignition and smiled. "Soon we'll know if it was worth the wait. It took ten years to get here, but that may not be all bad."

She waited for him to continue as she slipped her arms into her coat.

"You've heard what they say about appreciating things more the longer you hold out for them?"

She nodded. "Remember when we used to imagine this? When we talked about the different rides we'd heard about from our English friends?"

"Yup."

She pressed her palms on her thighs, sat up a little, and checked her pockets to make sure the money she'd brought from selling fresh vegetables last summer was still intact.

He chuckled. "Now we'll know if they exaggerated." Levi stuffed his keys into his back pocket and stepped out of the car. The moment Annie fastened the top of her coat, her door was opened.

She smiled her appreciation. *"Denke."*

Stepping toward the park, she loosened her neck scarf. "Nice day. Maybe I didn't need this after all."

"And the perfect company," he added. "I think God planned it this way. In fact, He's probably rewarding us for our long wait. But before we go any farther . . ."

They stopped at the same time and she looked up at him expectantly.

He rocked back and forth once on his heels. "You've got to promise me one thing." His eyes sparkled with amusement. In the bright light, they took on a deeper shade of green than hazel. Jade even. She couldn't take her eyes off the beautiful hue.

"What?"

He took her shoulders. "That today you'll have the best time in your entire life."

Doing a tiptoe dance, she responded with a big, agreeable nod. "You've got my word!"

As the sun brightened in the sky, Annie blinked to adjust her vision. Levi motioned to the structures in the distance. Even far away, shouts and screams filled the air. Tall, fast rides loomed before them. She pushed her hair back over her ears. It felt good to wear it loose.

The expression on Levi's face took on an appreciative look. There was a long silence between them before he spoke. "Your hair looks great down." He paused. "I always wondered how long it was. In fact, Annie, you're beautiful. From head to toe."

Slightly embarrassed by his approval, she changed the subject. She wasn't used to compliments on her looks and wasn't sure how to react. "You think it will still be exciting now that we're all grown up?"

He eyed her with a combination of amusement and protest. "Who says we're grown up?"

She widened her smile.

"And even if we are, what does it matter?" He threw up his hands. "We're here." He breathed in a deep, satisfied sigh.

They stepped around a mother pushing two kids in a stroller. As they passed, Annie wondered if that would be her someday. Children were a huge responsibility. Right now she only baked sponge cakes. As a mamma, she'd have to expand her talent as a cook. By the look of it, that mamma had her hands full. The little boy and little girl were practically hanging out of the stroller, pointing and chattering, while the out-of-breath woman pushed them, warning them to sit down.

As they made their way around, Annie gave a small wave. "Hello."

The young mom smiled and returned the gesture, while the youngsters squirmed.

When the family had gone on their way Annie realized Levi was waiting for a response to his last comment. "Advantages? What do you mean?" She quickened her pace to catch up with him.

He darted her a wry smile. "We're older."

She glanced at him as he took her arm to pull her away from a dip in the ground. When he released his gentle hold on her, she pressed him to continue. "Of course."

"That means, my friend, that we should appreciate what's right in front of us. Just think what we can do now that we couldn't ten years ago. Look at the advantages of coming right now instead of then."

She tried to see his point. After a few thoughtful moments, she nodded. "First of all, you wouldn't have been able to drive us here."

"My feet wouldn't have reached the accelerator or the brake."

They both laughed.

"True."

"And now we can be independent." He turned to better see her face. "I mean, just think how lucky we are not to have adults watching over us and telling us where to be and what time to meet. We can go on whatever rides we want without asking. That's got to count for something."

"You've got a point. And just think how fortunate we are that I can run around!" She motioned to her jeans and tennis shoes. "I can't imagine walking so far in my dress and hard black shoes. So that's another blessing."

"And in your jeans you seem . . ."

She waited for him to go on.

"English."

She giggled with excitement.

"On the outside, you're English, but on the inside, you're still my Amish girl."

She pointed a finger to establish her agreement. "You've got a point, Mr. Miller."

He rolled his eyes in amusement. "I don't look forward to the day when people call me 'Mr. Miller.'"

She frowned. "Why not? Miller's a nice enough name. And it's not hard to spell." She shrugged as an afterthought. "In fact, I like it."

"I suppose it's not bad."

"But wouldn't you rather be called by your first name? I mean . . ."

He harrumphed. "When people start referring to you with titles, it seems so formal. Like you're . . ." He hesitated. "Old."

"It does not!"

He lowered his voice. "Oh, but it does."

"Levi, that's all in your head. And you've got to get over it. What people call you really doesn't matter."

He raised a defensive hand. "I disagree. How people address you says everything. I don't know how you can think otherwise."

She stopped, planted both feet firmly together, and crossed her arms over her chest. He did the same and faced her.

"I *know* it doesn't matter."

"There goes my Annie, speaking her mind."

A short silence ensued while they stared at each other. Several moments later, they broke into laughter. "Such a serious discussion we're having."

The pitch of Annie's voice lifted to a more determined tone. "Levi, how you feel is all about how you act. I don't care if you're older than me."

Stepping quickly to keep up with him, she waved a hand to make her point. "If you do young things, you'll feel young. On the other hand, if you act like you're eighty, you'll feel ancient. It makes sense, right?"

He eyed her with skepticism. The flecks in his eyes did a doubtful dance.

"Okay, so I didn't convince you." She considered what she'd just said and contemplated how to substantiate it. With the snap of her fingers, her tone took on new enthusiasm. "Take Old Sam, for example. Do you consider him old?"

Levi pressed his lips together thoughtfully and darted her an undecided glance. Interestingly, she noticed the brown rims around his pupils had darkened again. *It happens every time he gets serious about something.*

Finally, he conceded, "No. You've got me there. I hate to let you win this one, but you have a point."

She gave a firm nod. "I've read that age is all a state of mind and I agree."

"Let's get something clear: I'm not admitting I agree with you. Just because Sam is in his eighties and I don't consider him old doesn't mean acting a certain age applies to everyone else. Old Sam is different. You agree, right?"

"*Jah*."

"Everyone else his age who doesn't act the way he does still seems old." When she started to protest, he held up a hand to stop her. "What I'm sure of is this: Anyone can have fun. If . . ." He hesitated.

"What?" From the side of her eye, Annie noted the careless roll of his eyes.

"Oh, it's nothing."

"Then tell me."

His cheeks had turned a light shade of pink. Then the color deepened.

"You're blushing!"

He wiped at his face, as if trying to rid the shade that had now spread to his ears. "No, I'm not."

She giggled. "*Jah*. You are. And now I *have* to know what you were about to say." She wagged a finger at him. "There's no way out of this one, so don't even try."

He took an irritated breath. "You know what I don't like about you, Ms. Annie?"

The corners of Annie's lips suddenly dropped.

He didn't give her a chance to respond. "That you can read my mind."

She sighed her relief and touched her hand to her chest. For a moment, she closed her eyes to regain her composure.

"I couldn't hide anything from you, even if I wanted to. Not only are you the most straightforward person I've ever met but, interestingly, you're also the most intuitive." He shook his head in defeat. "What I was about to say was that you can have fun anytime in your life . . ." His voice cracked with emotion. "As long as you're with your favorite person." He slowed his pace to gaze into her eyes.

Salty tears of joy immediately sprang to her eyes as she considered his touching words. She blinked in reaction to the sting. His honest confession nearly took her breath away and she had to stop to catch it.

He faced her so their eyes were locked together. His tone softened. "You're crying."

"I . . . I'm sorry."

Annie scolded herself silently. What was wrong with her? Before she had time to decide, he pulled her to his chest. Struggling to calm her chaotic emotions, she relished in the comforting hardness of his upper body. Even with her coat on, his forearms were as hard as boards. She breathed in the woodsy scent of his coat. The smell reminded her of a forest full of tall, strong oaks and large pines. Of leaves dropping from the trees and piling on the ground. She was fully aware that being close to him like this wasn't proper. But again, it felt right. She wouldn't be able to express her feelings to him once he was gone.

For blissful moments she closed her eyes and allowed herself to enjoy how protected he made her feel. The sensation was of pure comfort. Of not thinking about anything besides their unique relationship. No doubt Levi would make sure she was never harmed. When they were so close, she knew with each breath she took that he had her back. As a youngster, she'd experienced the same reassurance.

She sniffed back tears and wiped moisture from her face. Suddenly realizing how ridiculous she'd acted, she smiled a little and offered an embarrassed shrug. "I didn't mean to act like that."

The brown around his pupils was the darkest she'd ever seen it.

Feeling the need to explain her crazy, uncalled-for behavior, she went on, trying to look at him, "At first, when you said there was something you didn't like about me . . ."

"You're sensitive. But you know I'd never say anything to hurt you."

A nervous laugh escaped her. "The impact that statement had on me . . . I don't know how to explain it. But then, when you said you could have fun as long as you were with me . . ." She exhaled on a happy breath of relief. "It makes me feel *gut*."

"But you must have known that."

She nodded. "But hearing the words means so much. Just listen to me rattle on." As if on cue, they made their way inside the fence and joined the long ticket line.

The noise level was high. Between the screams echoing from the rides to the shoulder-to-shoulder people hustling from one place to another to kids and adults talking and laughing, serious conversation was difficult.

But reality had brought a strange sensation to Annie. The impact of Levi's *favorite-person* admission had taken her breath away. Inside, she'd always known how much she meant to him, hadn't she? So what on earth was the matter now? And why had she reacted with such great emotion? What he'd just told her would always be in her heart.

As they moved forward in the ticket queue, a kid ran past her, almost knocking her over.

"Whoa!" With a quick reaction, Levi steadied her. "You okay?"

"Jah."

As they waited, Annie heard the couple in front of them excitedly talking about which ride to go on first. When they would eat. Where. To her amusement, the girl pulled a list from her pocket with their schedule.

People behind them complained about the wait. To the side, a teenager ran after a group of kids, shouting as he did so.

The sun beat down on Annie's back; finally, she succumbed to the unusually warm October day and removed her scarf. She rolled it up as tightly as she could and stuffed it into her coat pocket.

Without thinking, she compared the wild, loud feeling of this amusement park to her country home. She smiled, wondering what her sister would think of this place. Arthur had never experienced such loud noise, even when the town got lots of visitors every Labor Day at the Cheese Festival. But the thrill rides made for a different kind of ambience. One she would want to visit but not live near.

The air was filled with a mélange of delicious smells. People walked shoulder-to-shoulder eating treats like oversize pretzels.

When Annie eyed Levi, her heart warmed. His special words had etched themselves into her heart: *As long as you're with your favorite person.* That meant she was his. A combination of emotions floated through her chest until she thought she would burst with happiness. She was Levi's number one. He must know that he was definitely hers.

As they stepped forward, Levi glanced at her blue jeans. "If I didn't know better, I'd think you had worn them your whole life. How do they feel?"

She pointed to the legs. "These?"

When he nodded, the corners of his lips lifted with amusement. She tried not to grin, fully aware that he was playing with her. He liked to hear her admit things she appreciated about the English.

She shrugged and acted as if she couldn't decide. She could tease, too. And she enjoyed his struggles. Finally, she nodded. "I like them. They're different. I thought they wouldn't be comfy. But turns out . . ." She threw up her hands in a helpless gesture. "I actually prefer them to dresses."

Levi lifted a confident chin. "That's music to my ears. The girl has some English taste in her."

They laughed.

Suddenly self-conscious, she lowered her eyes.

He glanced at her denim-covered legs again and narrowed his brows. He pressed his lips together and put his finger to his chin. Finally, he grinned mischievously. "Actually, you look fit. If I didn't know better, I'd think you exercised."

She smiled wider and ran her hands over the comfortable fabric that outlined her legs. "That's the first time I've ever heard anyone say that." A giggle escaped her.

"You're a bundle of positive energy with beautiful, honey-blond hair."

"I get why you enjoy a lot of the English perks." He looked at her.

Trying to read the expression in his eyes, she swallowed a knot in her throat as she guessed what he was feeling. In a tone that was a combination of happiness and surprise, she lowered her voice. "You miss being Amish, don't you?"

He turned so she couldn't glimpse his expression. Before he could respond, they were admitted into the park and the guy operating the Ferris wheel motioned them forward and opened the bar for them to step inside an orange seat. Beside him, Annie looked at Levi and furrowed her brows. "You ready for this?"

She shivered in delight. "I'll find out if I'm afraid of heights!"

With a jolt, their seat moved upward in a circular motion. Levi's hand clasped hers in a tight, reassuring grip. Behind them, kids were screaming.

Above, an airplane left a trail of white in the sky. For a moment, the sun disappeared behind a fluffy white cloud before reappearing in all its glory. Annie held her breath as the wheel stopped for a couple to get off and another to come on.

"We've got the best seats in the house!" He motioned. "Just look."

The view in front of them prompted Annie to draw in a surprised breath. "There are enough folks here to fill the state of Illinois." In silence, she took in the whirlwind of activity beneath them. She was so taken in by all the activity, she temporarily forgot her initial fear.

When they stopped again, their metal seat swung back and forth. Annie held onto the bar that locked them in with her right hand while Levi held her left. After another slight jolt, the wheel moved again.

Squeaking noises floated through the air as they moved up in a slow pace. Annie looked at Levi from her peripheral vision. A warm appreciation filled her heart as she recalled their long-ago dream. However, her instincts told her that he was doing this for her. After all, he could come to amusement parks any day he wanted. He had access to a vehicle. And a driver's license.

The Ferris wheel made a full, continuous circle. The second time around, their seat stopped at the very top. Annie drew in a deep, uncertain breath. She had never been up this high. But she was okay with it, though at this point she was sure she didn't like heights. But something inside her whispered for her to enjoy it.

She closed her eyes and said a quick prayer for safety. When she opened them, a new sense of security swept through her, where the comforting sensation lingered.

When the wheel moved again, she smiled at Levi. "Aren't we lucky?"

"Because we're here?"

"Uh-huh. I love everything about today. I don't ever want it to end."

"Me neither."

To their right, a roller coaster soared up and down the tracks. Screams floated through the park. Above, a giant balloon hovered. Annie wondered if the person inside it enjoyed the view as much as she did.

Before today, she'd never been on a ride. It wasn't

so much the thrill she was enjoying; it was the grand view. She was in a moving lookout tower.

It amazed her that God had this kind of front-row seat of the entire universe. And He saw everything, good and bad. What was even more incredible was that He knew what each person was going to do before they did it. The knowledge that God had so much power, and that He was full of love and forgiveness, was overwhelming.

When the ride ended, Levi helped her out of the seat. "Where to next?"

She eyed him with uncertainty. "It's your call."

He raised a curious brow. "You like pirates?"

She giggled.

"I'll take that as a yes. Pirate's Flight, here we come!"

Several rides later, they shared a bench on the grounds. Annie stretched her legs and sighed happily. "Oh, Levi, this is everything I dreamed it would be. Even better."

"Because you're English for the day . . ."

She grinned at the way his brows scrunched when he said the words.

"We didn't bring sunblock," he said, eyeing her forehead.

"I'll be okay. I suppose you don't have to worry about burning."

"Fortunately not. I inherited my dad's dark complexion. I tan easily."

She waited for him to continue.

"As you know, I spend summers outside, working on houses. Roofing. Guttering. Painting. Siding. Even landscaping. All that stuff."

"Which do you enjoy most?"

Levi pressed his lips together in a straight line. "I've never really thought about it. But if I had to choose, it would be laying stonework above fireplaces."

She considered the admission. "That requires creativity. It's a talent."

They got up at the same time and automatically proceeded to the next ride. As they waited in the queue, he replied, "Now that you mention it, yeah. I love choosing where to place the rocks so when the project's finished, it looks like a finished puzzle. And that each stone was meant to go where it is. Of course there's nothing as satisfying as admiring the finished product. There's something so rewarding about knowing someone's going to enjoy the thought and planning that went into building a place."

A loud cry startled them. They both looked to the side, where a kid had fallen and scraped his knee. The child's father quickly picked him up while the mother pulled a Band-Aid from her oversize bag.

A smile lifted the corners of Annie's lips. "I'm really proud of you and what you've become. And working with your dad? It's great that you two get along so well. It must be every boy's dream to partner with his father. You think that'll happen?"

He shrugged. "It already has. I mean, we do every project together. Some things I'm faster at, like masonry stuff. Dad's better at laying drywall. Overall, when we work together, everything seems to get done pretty seamlessly. I'm making great strides at creating the overall picture from scratch. But no one does it like Dad."

They stepped forward as the line ahead of them became shorter. He looked down before continuing. "As far as planning the entire idea on paper and coming up with a price, he's the pro. Dad bids for the materials. And it isn't as easy as it looks. There's way more to it than meets the eye. But he's taught me everything I know."

She took in his proud expression. "When we were kids, you drew me pictures of the houses you wanted to build. And it's interesting that you had the very notion of putting up your own house when you were this high." She raised her hand above her waist to estimate.

He nodded.

"Now here you are, Levi, helping your dad build beautiful mansions. I would love to see your work sometime."

They were quiet for a moment. When Levi spoke, emotion edged his voice. "Someday, Annie, I want to show you my world. Drive you around in Dad's truck so you can see what I do."

She didn't respond. With all her heart she wanted to take him up on his offer, but at the same time, she knew it would never happen. What was she going to do? Take a horse and buggy to Morton? She doubted horses were permitted on the interstate. Besides, she was fully aware of the limits on her relationship with the wonderful man beside her. They were of marrying age. Because of that, she had to let him go. Her lips slipped a notch in disappointment.

As they moved forward in the line, he raised his voice to be heard above the screaming and yelling. "Dad's proud to have me with him."

"Did he tell you that?"

Levi shook his head. "No, but it shows. I see it in his eyes. Hear it in his voice. He loves when we're riding in the truck together. In fact, I think he's living his dream by us working together." Levi cleared his throat. "But I have my own dream, Annie."

She waited.

"Building my own home. A two-story." He looked off in the distance. When he spoke again, he moved his hands in front of him, as if making a visual of his thought. "I can see the circular stairwell with a beautiful dark oak banister. A double-sided gas fireplace. Granite countertops throughout the kitchen. And large gray stones above the fireplace."

Annie swished her hand to chase away a fly that had appeared in front of her. She wasn't sure why, but her heart had sunk a couple of notches. She silently scolded herself. This was her best friend. She should be happy he had such goals. And she was. She forced a smile. What made her sad was that she wouldn't be part of his bright, wonderful future. Finally, she was ready to admit it. In the back of her mind she'd known it. But for the first time she officially acknowledged it. Her shoulders sagged. She lowered her chin. After Levi left there would be no more trips to Six Flags. No more conversations about dreams. Still, she was happy to be with him while she could.

He turned closer to tip her chin up with his finger. His voice was edged with concern. "Hey. What's wrong?"

She remained silent. Maybe it was better not to broach the devastating reality. Then, as usual, she decided on honesty. "I was thinking about our friendship." She took a deep, desperate breath. "Levi, does it have to end? Just because we live in different towns . . ."

The tan circles around his pupils darkened even more. In fact, the color had changed so drastically, the brown shade was almost black. His tone was more serious than usual as he pushed her chin up another notch with his finger.

When a man motioned to them, they stepped quickly onto a seat. The bar in front of them locked into place. As they started to move up into the air, Levi continued their conversation. "Annie, I'll always be here for you. No matter that we attend different churches. Or towns. You'll be my best friend forever. And no one can stop it. Deal?"

Her lips relaxed before lifting into a big smile. "Deal."

Their gazes were locked in mutual understanding as their bench stopped in midair. But even though they were higher than she'd ever been, Annie's focus was on what he'd just told her. "Suddenly, everything looks wonderful again. I couldn't stand the thought of you leaving, but when you put it like that, how can I be disappointed?"

His smile was sympathetic. "I don't want you to be unhappy. Ever. I'm going to make sure that every moment I spend with you will be a memory I can go to whenever I'm lonely."

"Do you keep a journal, too?"

He shrugged. "Sort of. But it's not in writing." His lips curved mischievously. "That's to my benefit 'cause no one can find it and read it."

She sighed as the ride stopped and a man released the bar in front of them. As they stepped out into the main area, he told Annie, "I store all the good times in my mind. They're like chapters in a book."

She pressed her lips together thoughtfully as their steps slowed. "Okay, Levi. That's certainly a unique way to keep a journal. What about the bad?"

He shook his head. "Why try to remember them? It's a waste of time. God didn't put us on this earth forever. I'm sure He wants us to make the most of our days. And focusing on things you'd rather forget would be a poor investment of time, don't you think?"

She considered his words and finally nodded. "I like your take on that. And it makes sense. So . . . today: You'll store it in a mental chapter?"

He offered a quick nod.

"Then I need to know how you'll decide which chapter. I want you to make sure you remember, so you can find it without any trouble. And I want you to revisit it often. So will I. Of course my journal is in writing. Today is like a good book that I'll want to read over and over." She crossed her hands over her chest and breathed in with excitement. "I never want to forget this."

His eyes sparkled. "How many rides have we been on?"

They counted on their fingers. "Six."

"That decides it. Today is chapter six." He winked. "I'll bookmark it for easy reference."

She giggled. "I'd never considered life experiences as book chapters before. But they are, really. And you're right about focusing on the good ones.

After all, why on earth would anyone reread a bad story?"

He shrugged. "They wouldn't. But you keep a journal? A real one?"

She gave careful consideration to his question. It wasn't as if she didn't have an answer. It was just that she'd never shared that she kept a journal with anyone. Of course she wasn't as close to anyone else as she was to Levi. But he'd shared that he kept a mental journal with her, and there was no reason to hide anything from him. In fact, the more she thought about it, the more she realized she very much wanted to talk to him about it.

They walked past more rides, food stands, and games, trying to talk above the noise. She nodded. "*Jah.* I started when Old Sam gave me a hope chest."

"He's really fond of you, isn't he?"

She gave her eyes a happy roll. "I make sure he has a steady supply of sponge cakes."

"Obviously he appreciates that."

She nodded. "I write in my journal every night. But mine's different from yours. Before I go to bed each night, I like to rethink the things that happened during the day. How they affected me. Sometimes I'm not sure how to see things, but as soon as I study them in writing, everything becomes clear. I jot down what's important, what I don't want to forget when I'm old. I don't even try to ignore something I don't like; I write about the good and the bad. Things that worry me. What makes me happy. It's funny, but sometimes I don't know how I truly feel until the words are on paper."

"So your journal's kind of like a therapy." He

paused, then reworded. "It helps you get things straight in your head?"

"Uh-huh. Because life's about both good and bad. I like it that you just store the happy times. I wish that worked for me. But for some reason I have to walk myself through every moment to figure out how I think it will all play out in the end. And I love storing my thoughts in Old Sam's beautiful chest. He even engraved a sponge cake recipe on the lid. And the wood smells so good."

"Like oak?"

She nodded. "I keep the lid open while I write to glance at the recipe and to enjoy the woodsy scent. It's comforting."

"So the chest really has a special place in your heart."

She considered his words before acknowledging their truth with a nod. "It's a place to store my dreams. And *jah*, the chest is very special. Just like my thoughts. I don't share my sentiments with anyone but you and Old Sam. So, in a way, the journal's kind of a sounding board. You have a thinking place, maybe?"

He darted her an expression that was difficult to read. "Can you keep a secret?"

"You know I can." Her heart pumped to an excited beat. Levi was going to confide in her again, tell her something he trusted her to keep confidential. That he would tell her something private made her feel important.

"I do have what you would call a 'thinking place.'"

She waited for him to go on, nearly losing her footing when a couple of kids bumped her. Levi was quick to steady her, and she thanked him. He resumed their conversation. "Like my journal, it's a place I go in my mind when I want to relax. And when I need to make important decisions."

"So . . . it's like me heading to my journal in my hope chest."

"Yes." He rolled his shoulders before meeting her gaze.

Her chest rose and fell to an anxious beat as their gazes locked.

Finally, he spoke in what was barely more than a whisper. "It's Pebble Creek."

Chapter Seven

Two hours later, as sunlight still warmed the amusement park, Annie and Levi sat down in front of a large water fountain. As the water spewed upward and landed into a small pond, Levi thought about what he'd told Annie. Unexpectedly, a deep sigh of relief escaped his lungs. Finally, he'd admitted it verbally. After many years, he'd finally confessed it out loud.

For some strange reason, he wondered why it had taken this long to acknowledge that Pebble Creek was his mental haven. It didn't make sense. After all, Pebble Creek was a painful reminder of his father's shunning. It was a part of his upbringing he'd struggled to put behind him.

He decided to talk more about it with Annie. Maybe she could help him understand how something he wanted to forget had actually become a place he treasured.

"Annie, I know it probably won't make sense to you . . ."

"What?"

"That Pebble Creek would be the special place I treasure. It doesn't make sense to me either."

She frowned. "I'm not sure I understand. Why on earth would it not be? Pebble Creek is the most beautiful spot in the world. The place where we became best friends."

He shrugged and gave her question more thought. "Because in the whole scheme of things, it's connected to the shunning. A part of my past I'd rather not remember. It's complicated. It's like I can't forget the shunning without pushing Pebble Creek under the rug. Trust me; I've tried. But I haven't been able to put it behind me."

Annie's voice bordered on enthusiasm. "That's because you really don't want to." She hesitated. "Levi, as you said, life's complicated. Not everything can be black and white. You've always had a special place in your heart for that land. No matter how hard you try, there's no way you can put something behind you that you love with everything you have."

"But remember what I told you about keeping only good chapters in my mind?"

She nodded. "Maybe you could look at it as a great scene in a bad chapter?"

He sighed. "Pebble Creek is a large part of my life." His voice was emotional. "It's where we used to hang out. Where we dreamed up all sorts of stuff we'd do when we got older."

He hesitated, trying to translate thoughts into words. "For years I've struggled to erase Pebble Creek from my memory to help me forget what happened. I mean . . ." He lifted his hands in a helpless gesture. "Let's face it: That's a treacherous chapter. A place I never want to revisit."

She smiled. As he watched the corners of her lips lift, he swallowed a sudden lump in his throat. He wasn't sure he wanted to deal with this unexpected emotion, but he saw Annie was waiting for him to continue.

She pressed her lips into a thoughtful line. "Levi, I understand why you're torn."

"I knew you would. 'Cause you're a problem solver. So . . . what do I do?"

She squinted down at the ground before leveling his gaze with hers. "I'm not sure. I guess it's up to you to decide." The expression in her eyes was hard to read.

"Are you kidding?"

"No. Let me put it this way: Do you really want to forget everything associated with the shunning?"

He contemplated what she'd said.

While she changed positions, Annie waited before responding until a group of women speaking a different language passed by. "Think about it, Levi. Sure, Pebble Creek is connected to what happened to your dad. But so are other things. Take, for instance, little Jake. And your aunt and uncle." She lowered her voice. "And me. When you get right down to it, I'm a large part of your past. Do you want to forget me?"

He rolled his eyes. "That's a no-brainer. Of course not." A knot that was a combination of happiness and sadness formed in his chest and he placed a gentle hand over the ache to rub it. But, to his chagrin, it wouldn't go away. Nor would the shunning. How could he escape what bothered him?

Several thoughtful moments passed. Finally, Annie said, "Levi, I understand what you're saying. But in the end, you're Levi Miller. So even if I tried, I couldn't tell you how to cope. All I can do is explain how I would handle it. And why."

He waved a hand for her to go on. "I'm listening."

She crossed her legs and rested them against the bench. She clasped her hands together on her lap and flexed her fingers while she turned to better face him. "Remember what I told you about writing everything in my journal? Good and bad? Because exploring the whole picture is the only way I can decide how I feel?"

He nodded.

"When you said you only store good chapters in your mind, I wondered how you did it."

He started to interrupt, but she stepped in before he could continue.

"To me, it's impossible. Because life will always be a combination of good and bad. When you get right down to it, there's no way to have one without the other." A laugh escaped her. "Have you ever read a book with just good chapters?"

He shook his head.

"Of course, not. Because there aren't any." She raised her hands to the bright blue sky in a helpless gesture. "Levi, you can't skip the bad parts in life."

He dropped his palms to his thighs. "I didn't mean I planned to go through life only remembering happy things. What I said was that I preferred to delete what's bad from my mind. And only remember what's good."

She drew her brows together and nodded slowly. "I get it. But that's impossible." She shrugged. "Because when you put everything together, good memories—or chapters"—she grinned—"come from bad ones."

He looked at her to clarify.

"Okay. Let me think of an example."

Levi watched her with keen interest as her mouth pressed into a determined line. She was trying so hard to help him.

Several heartbeats later, she sat up straight and patted her legs with her fingers. "I think I have an example. It has to do with Old Sam."

"Why am I not surprised?" he teased her.

She took a decisive breath. "Okay." She leaned forward to lift one leg over the other. "You weren't here when Sam's wife passed away, but I remember hearing the news as if it happened yesterday."

He tapped his foot to a nervous beat.

"After he lost her, Sam . . . he wasn't himself."

Levi raised a doubtful brow.

Annie raised a hand in protest. "I know it's hard to imagine Sam quiet and avoiding others, but that's pretty much what happened. He even lost a lot of weight." She shrugged. "That's why I started taking him sponge cakes. At first, he thanked me of course. But other than that, he didn't say much."

He chuckled. "The Sam I remember was quite a talker."

She nodded in agreement. "It was a while before he invited me into his big red barn. In fact, that's when he started designing award-winning hope chests. I think creating beautiful designs helped him deal with his loss. He'd pour out his heart as he worked on them. And even though I lacked the experience to help him, I listened." She swallowed.

As the sun slipped behind a cloud, a cool breeze prompted Annie to wrap her arms around her midsection. She tapped her foot to a quick beat. "As the days passed, things started looking up. He wasn't as serious. And when I sat with him, he talked about things other than Esther. He chatted about what went on in the community. I was relieved at the sudden change. I had started to doubt it would happen. But it did. Sam started to make the most amazing hope chests I'd ever seen. And when he did, it was like Esther was helping him from above. His work started to win awards. Suddenly, there were so many orders, he wondered if he could keep up with them. But amazingly, he did. And his work . . ." Annie closed her eyes for a moment and drew her hands over her heart. When she looked at Levi again, moisture had formed in her eyes, reminding Levi of the early morning dew on his mother's geraniums in the summertime.

She blinked. "It was as if Esther's death had inspired him."

He cupped his chin with his hand. "Poor guy. I didn't realize he'd had it so hard."

"I've told you about the gift he made me. Levi, I know I'm partial to Sam, but he's incredible. The soft flannel lining fascinates me. And the sponge cake recipe on the lid?" She drew in a breath and pushed it out again. "Every letter is a work of art. But you know what I love most about it?"

He shook his head.

"That he thought enough of me to create it. Not only did he give it to me to keep precious things inside but he even went as far as to take something that's a part of me—my sponge cakes—and carve the entire recipe into the oak. That was a special touch."

She paused, wondering if she was making sense. She raised her chin a notch to better meet Levi's gaze. "Do you see what I'm saying about both bad and good playing a role in our lives?"

"You mean that if something bad hadn't happened—in other words, the loss of Sam's wife—your hope chest wouldn't have materialized. And neither would your special relationship with Old Sam."

She offered a satisfied nod. "We know the shunning was devastating. It's a hard thing to get over. And you probably won't."

"It's stuck with me forever, unfortunately."

"Of course. But Levi, there has to be a reason it happened. Something good must result from it."

He cocked his head in a thoughtful manner to digest what she'd said. A little girl running from her mamma bumped him and quickly apologized. Levi smiled at her in response. "Annie, I like the way you see things. I really do. You're good for me."

Her eyes danced at his compliment.

"And I'm sure that, most of the time, things do happen for a purpose. But the shunning?" He gave a slow shake of his head. "When it comes to that . . .

Ten years have passed and nothing even close to good has happened because of it."

She lowered her voice. "Just think of Old Sam."

"I wonder if he accepts that his loss is part of the plan."

"He trusts the Lord."

"Speaking of plans . . . I have something in mind for lunch."

Annie giggled. "You do?"

He waggled a finger. "Yup. And it's something special."

She grinned. The sun hit the beauty mark just beneath her right eye and his stomach did an unexpected somersault. He used to tease her about that freckle. Now that she was grown, it had taken on a whole different meaning. In a good way.

"There's something I want you to try. And it may very well turn out to be one of your all-time favorite foods."

"Like chicken and dumplings?"

He laughed. "Kind of. You ever heard of corn dogs?"

She offered an excited nod. "They sell them every year at the Cheese Festival."

He snapped his fingers. "I thought it would be something new for you."

She opened her arms. "This whole adventure at Six Flags is new to me. Just because I've eaten a corn dog before . . ."

He gave a slow shake of his head. "But my treat won't be a surprise." With one swift motion, he stood and smiled down at her. "I'll have to change gears. Let's go for something else."

She stood and clutched his wrists. "No! I love corn dogs. In fact . . ." Her lips curved into a mischievous grin. "I was looking forward to one even before we came here."

"Ah ha. Now I know the real reason you wanted to come."

"Levi, can I ask you something?"

"You know the answer."

"Okay. It has to do with Pebble Creek. The shunning. Everything, really."

He waited for her to continue.

"I know you can never look at the Amish church with the fondness you did when we were kids. And I understand."

"I know you do, Annie. You seem to understand everything about me. But what's your question?"

The concerned expression on her face made him even more curious. "You're sad."

She waved a hand in front of her. "No. No! Everything about this day is wonderful. But I wish you hadn't experienced what you did with the shunning." She breathed a heavy sigh. "You see, I'm Amish. And because I long for happy endings . . ."

She threw her hands up in the air, then dropped them to her sides. "I want you to feel good about the Amish." She closed her eyes and made fists with her hands. "I want it so much it hurts." She opened her eyes. "Because that's me. Levi, we were happy kids. There's surely a part of you that misses the faith that's so dear to me."

He considered her honesty. As he watched her, listened to her sincerity, his heart warmed. For long moments he gazed into her eyes. He was fully aware that she expected a reply, but he couldn't get out the words. It was as if the beautiful girl in front of him had grabbed hold of his heart and wouldn't let go. He knew how hard it was going to be to go back home without her. He was feeling emotional again, and now he felt something he'd never experienced before, in a way that made him more vulnerable than he'd ever been in his life.

"Levi? Are you okay?"

He forced a smile. "I was . . . just . . . thinking." He squared his shoulders and raised his chin. "What I miss about the Amish life? I think I have an answer."

She waited patiently.

"I miss the quiet."

"Jah?"

"When we changed churches, I had a difficult time adjusting to the noise. You know, all the electronics. The television. The radio and such. I really miss the quiet."

"I think I would miss that, too."

"But, Annie, that's not what I miss most about the Amish life." He wondered how to put his thoughts into words. "There's something about the Amish life I miss more than anything in the world. And I don't know how I can go through life without it."

Her voice was so soft, he could barely hear her. "Tell me what it is."

"It's you."

It wasn't any easier finding the car in the full parking lot than it had been finding an empty spot in the morning. The temperature had dropped a few degrees since they'd arrived, and the cool breeze pushed Levi's jacket flat to his back.

Long honey-brown strands of hair waved against Annie's cheeks. She giggled as Levi took her hand and they quickened their pace.

Finally, the car was in front of them. He pushed the automatic opener and the lock clicked. Motioning to her, he opened Annie's door.

"Thanks."

"My pleasure."

Inside, he pulled a large piece of cotton candy from the stick in her hand. He turned the ignition and flipped the heat on low. As the air blew out of the vents, Annie held the snack between them. When they finished the last bite, Annie wrapped the white cone holder in the plastic bag and put it down on the floor behind her. The sweet, addictive smell lingered and the delicious taste was still on Levi's tongue as he licked his lips. The treat had been the perfect ending to a perfect day.

He breathed a sigh that was a combination of joy and regret as he pulled onto the highway. Happiness because of the wonderful day. Disappointment that it was ending.

Checking the rearview mirror, he slowed for another car to pull ahead of him. Levi didn't mind the silence. In fact, it was comforting.

As he glimpsed Annie from the corner of his eye, he opened his mouth to ask her what she'd thought of Six Flags. But when he noted her calm, satisfied demeanor, he decided not to disturb the moment. There was no need to inquire if she'd enjoyed the park. He knew it. He could tell it from the way her lips lifted slightly at the corners. Contentment emanated from her thin, fit-looking body, and from the relaxed way she sat with her legs crossed and the flushed expression of happiness in her rosy cheeks.

It was hard for him to look away. Strands of thick hair fell over her shoulders. With the honey-blond mass down, her face looked a couple of years older. She was even more beautiful than before. He swallowed and silently chastised himself for being so taken in with her appearance.

But that wasn't the only thing about her that was attractive. He admired her sensitivity, her honesty, and her straightforward manner. In fact, he was downright impressed by everything about her. He tried to imagine someone else just like her. Someone English. The thought prompted his smile to droop. He knew finding another Annie, English or Amish, would be impossible. When God had made her, He'd thrown away the mold.

Without words, they were comfortable with each other. That was part of what he loved about her. *Stop reading too much into her. I would never join the faith that shunned my father. And I'm pretty sure Annie will never become English.*

When he turned his attention back to the road, a complicated emotion swept through him. He wasn't sure what it was. What he did know was that it was edged with never-before-experienced excitement. The sensation made him warm inside. At the same time, it caused him to feel uncomfortable.

The sun began to disappear as a kaleidoscope

of beautiful colors flooded the western sky. The beautiful picture reminded Levi of a mélange of different colors dumped onto a thick, white canvas in art class. For some odd reason, he compared the sunset, with all its unique hues, to his emotions. He bit his lip with uncertainty. And he didn't like being unsure. The control chair was where he preferred to sit. But right now he found himself a member of the unsure club.

He pressed his lips together and darted another quick glance at Annie. His heart fluttered with an unknown sensation. The expression on her face reflected everything good. Happiness. Fulfillment. Everything that was the opposite of the unidentified chaos rushing through his veins. Annie could help him make sense of what was happening within him; he knew it. He opened his mouth to speak, but no words came out. Thank goodness.

How can I disturb her when she's at peace? And what's up with this weird feeling inside me?

Annie put a hand over her mouth to cover a yawn as she stepped into the kitchen. The moment she closed the door, the light flipped on. She stiffened. "Mamma. You're still up?"

She was quick to note the new small lines under her mother's eyes. In her blue night dress, she looked unusually small and fragile as she gave Annie a once-over. Suddenly, Annie felt rebellious in her English attire when, in fact, the outing hadn't been about that at all.

"Your dad and I worried all day about you." She embraced Annie in a tight, affectionate hug. "I'm glad you're home, safe and sound. That was a long trip. Was the park what you expected?"

Annie lifted her hands in the air in excitement. "It was amazing. But not tonight, Mamma. It's late. We'll get up early for chores. Don't worry; I'll tell you everything in the morning!"

Unable to contain her enthusiasm, a sudden rush of energy swept through Annie, and she lifted her chin. "It was fun, Mamma! The drive, the rides, the food . . . Levi is so good to me."

Annie's excitement was short-lived. She was quick to catch Mamma's lips press into a straight, doubtful line. Her words were edged with sympathy. "I'm glad you could do this before he leaves. This was the perfect ending to your time together."

The joyful sensation in Annie's stomach plummeted. Mamma's words quickly reminded her that her moments with Levi were at an end. Trying to hide her disappointment, she nodded. "God blessed us with this special day." She dropped her hands to her sides. "I'll never forget it. And I'll always be grateful."

Without saying good night, Annie stepped quickly to the stairs, where she tiptoed so she wouldn't awaken her dad or sister. At the same time, Mamma quietly slipped into her downstairs bedroom.

In her room, Annie stopped for a moment and closed her eyes. "Dear God, please help me to focus on the positive. Amen." When she opened her eyes again, she lit her lantern wick. The bright, welcoming light from the moon swept in through the large window and landed in a circle on the floor.

While Annie took off her jeans and T-shirt, a combination of emotions flitted through her. She rolled her shoulders to relax. With great care, she folded her English clothes and neatly placed them in a drawer. She raised a doubtful brow, wondering if she would ever wear them again; even if she didn't, she would save them to remind her of the day.

She gave the souvenirs a final glance and smiled a little before slipping her midnight-blue nightgown over her head. Then she moved to the window, pressed her palms on the sill, and stared with amazement at the Milky Way in the dark, clear sky.

The enticing aroma of homemade chicken and dumplings still filled the house. Annie regretted missing her mamma's best meal, but there were no regrets about her English day.

Suddenly, Annie tensed and her lips drooped. The expression on Mamma's face hadn't been happy when Annie had entered the house, but tomorrow, after they'd rested, Annie would tell her about the park. And the drive. Maybe that would ease her mind. She didn't understand why Mamma was so disapproving of her time with Levi. What on earth did she think? That she would run off with him?

Annie's wants were few, but she wished her folks had more faith in her. It didn't make sense for them to worry. After all, she'd never given them any reason not to trust her. It was disappointing that her outing had met with such unwarranted skepticism.

Today had been the best day of her life. With a deep, satisfied sigh, Annie pulled the journal from her hope chest. As she took in the engraved sponge cake recipe, chaotic emotions flitted through her mind. The bright beam from the full moon made it easy to see.

She got comfortable on the soft rug against her bed, crossing her feet at the ankles and wiggling her toes in delight. Her feet had easily acclimated to tennis shoes. And if she had her way, she would prefer to wear jeans rather than her dark dress to do chores. It was easier to bend and move her legs.

Looking down at the journal in her lap, Annie entered the date at the top right corner of a fresh page, then put her pen to the white-lined paper while drawing her brows together thoughtfully. Her heart had been anxiously waiting to pour out the details of the day.

I feel so many emotions, I don't know where to start. I just got home from Six Flags with Levi. A decade ago, we dreamed of going. Our English friends raved about how exciting it was. And it certainly didn't disappoint. In fact, the park lived up to its reputation in every way imaginable.

When we were kids, Levi promised me that when we did Rumspringa, *he'd take me there. Of course things have changed drastically since then. At that time, he hadn't planned to move away. He hadn't had an inkling that the very faith that bonded us would eventually separate us. Still, he kept his word. He promised me the best time of my life. And it was.*

She jotted down details about the long drive. Passing corn and bean fields. About parking. While she wrote down her thoughts, something nagged at her, a combination of excitement and fear. As hard as she tried to figure out what it was, she couldn't. She gave a gentle lift of her shoulders and focused on her journal.

We went on so many rides! The Apocalypse. The Bahama Blast. Even the carousel. A Ferris wheel! Bumper cars. We even took in a show with dancers and singers. They were so good.

The day wasn't cheap, and I was prepared for it. I brought money from the vegetable sales to cover my expenses. But I didn't pay a cent. Levi paid for everything. I offered to cover my half, but he wouldn't hear of it. He's such a kind person. And I love how he takes care of me. My favorite part of the day was a corn dog and homemade lemonade. They tasted delicious! Even better than at the Cheese Festival!

Levi and I picnicked on a wooden bench in the middle of the rides. It was pretty noisy for conversation, but I enjoyed the ambience and being with him.

When the moon slipped behind cloud cover, the room became darker. Annie blinked to adjust her eyes. Automatically, she got up and slid the lantern closer to where she sat. She reclaimed her position on the rug. As she put pen to paper, a big yawn escaped her. She closed her eyes for a moment.

When she opened them again, she continued her train of thought.

Throughout the day, one conversation kept replaying in my mind. I couldn't figure out why I couldn't let it go. But now I know why. Because he told me how he cares for me. He said he could be happy doing anything as long as I was with him.

For a blissful moment, she gazed up at the stars and the moon. If God could create such an amazing universe, surely He could have Levi's dad welcomed back into the community. Compared to creating the sun and the moon, wasn't forgiving Levi's dad with open arms simple? If only that were to happen, Levi's entire life would change. And so would hers.

As she pictured Levi, the corners of her lips tugged into a wide grin. They had discussed so many things in such a short time; it was difficult to process it all.

Despite the wonderful day, I find myself uneasy. Levi and I passed a mother struggling with two young children. Now I understand why the scene disturbed me. She prompted me to think of my own uncertain future.

Annie drew in a deep, uneasy breath and rested the journal and pen on her thighs. She stretched her legs and pressed the palms of her hands on the thick, soft rug. Why the uncertainty? She wasn't sure. She'd always known her goal in life was to have children. To raise a family. To work side by side with her husband. The typical Amish role of a woman. In fact, she'd never really considered other options. But right now, there was a problem. Adjusting to her writing position, she wrote again.

I try to picture myself with little ones, but I can't. Why not?

She tapped the end of her pen against the paper and pressed her lips together thoughtfully. Then took a deep breath. There. At least she'd written it down. Without hesitation, she continued her train of thought.

Raising a family is what I've most looked forward to. In fact, I planned to save my most special things in my hope chest to share with my children. But today I realized kids aren't first and foremost on my list for my future.

A surprised sigh escaped her lips.

The most important part of a family, to me, is a husband I truly love and respect. A man I can't live without.

That admission made her heart skip a beat. This was the first time she'd recognized that. Uncertainty trickled down her spine while she tried for words to better explain this change in philosophy.

My parents tell me getting married isn't about having that crazy, wonderful feeling I've read about in the pit of my stomach. To them, marriage is simply about growing old with someone you can count on to help with chores. With the kids. Someone who's there when you need a hand.

Annie took in the moonbeam that had slightly shifted on the floor. Salty tears stung her eyes and she blinked. Couldn't there be more to life? Was she expecting the impossible? She was a dreamer, after all. Or so she'd been told.

Is it wrong to want a man I think about night and day? As much as I want children, I can't picture them with a man who's simply dependable.

Her fingers stiffened and she pressed the pen a little harder. Looking down at her words etched them permanently into her mind.

Do I want too much? I would love a fairytale marriage like I've read about in novels at the library. Someone to float with into the sunset, laughing and talking of wondrous things.

Pointing her fingertip against her chin, she considered the eligible men in her community and bit her lip. There weren't many options. Most girls her age already had their eye on someone. Yet no one appealed to her. She couldn't imagine standing in front of a couple hundred people as Levi's cousin and Katie had, and acting excited about committing the rest of her life to any of the eligible bachelors. Her stomach ached. Suddenly, what energy she had evaporated.

I'm not sure who God has planned for me to marry.

She gave a casual shrug of her shoulders. A half smile of relief tugged at her lips.

Thank goodness, I don't have to decide this very moment. I shouldn't worry about things that are out of my control. I want to cherish each moment. And that's exactly what I did today. I enjoyed everything! Each moment seemed larger than life. I realize, though, that my happiness wasn't because of the rides. Or the food.

It was because I was with Levi.

She paused, wondering how to write in a few sentences what made him so special.

No one in my life has made me feel as important and as special as he has. There's something amazing about the way he treats me. Like everything I say is important. As if no one matters but me. When I'm with him, I reciprocate the way I feel.

I've wondered many times if I'm making too much of this. Here's proof I'm not: happiness and excitement fill his voice. He shares his inner thoughts with me. And no matter how much I talk, he doesn't forget anything I've told him; that means he pays attention, and he wouldn't if he didn't care about me. Most of all, I know I'm important to him by the sacrifices he makes. He asked special permission from my folks to take me to Six Flags. Before getting their approval, he answered so many questions and committed to keeping me safe. But he didn't stop with that. He bought me blue jeans and tennis shoes. And the price of the ticket and food?

If she could whistle, she would. The money he'd spent must have been his entire savings.

But the best part was when Levi told me he could have fun anywhere as long as he was with his favorite person.

She pushed out a deep, happy breath and looked up at the moonbeam in all its glory.

I'm his favorite person. When he said it, I teared up. Now that I've processed the importance of what he told me, I feel honored. Really, I can't think of anything that could make me happier. But it's more than that.

Annie straightened her back. She looked out her window and searched the sky to consider her thoughts. Longing to figure out what still troubled her.

If he thinks so highly of me, don't I have a responsibility to come through for him?

She pressed her lips together and long moments passed as she contemplated Levi Miller and her reaction to him.

When Levi actually said those words, I realized how important he is to me, too. I always knew it. But now I acknowledge it. And he is *my favorite person. I love being with him, and I'll miss him terribly for the rest of my life.*

She closed her eyes in agony. *The rest of her life* seemed a long time to be without her favorite person. Now she knew exactly why the struggling mamma had made her sad. She turned the page of her journal.

The image of the mamma saddened me because the only person I can picture myself pushing a stroller with is Levi.

Emotions raced in every direction, creating total chaos in her mind. She pressed the knot in the back of her neck to ease the ache, but it lingered. Just like a headache after the flu.

It wasn't easy, but she wrote it.

He's English; I'm Amish. But that's not the main issue. The very church I plan to join has let him down in a way that seems impossible to fix. When he talks about the shunning, I can sense his resentment. That's when I'm fully reminded that when it comes to religion, we're on two different teams. I'm not free to choose the man I want. In my heart I know that being with my favorite person forever can't happen. And that reality is causing me to be unhappy.

I can never, ever let anyone know how strongly I feel about him. It's wrong for me to want something I can't have. And I must nix those dangerous feelings right now. Before they go any further. Maybe it would have been better if he hadn't come back. If that were the case, there wouldn't be this turmoil inside me. Yet because of him, I had the best time of my life. What on earth is wrong with that? Why should I fear having a great, memorable day with my best friend?

I know why. It's because I have a responsibility to my faith. That means adhering to the Ordnung. *I heard our pastor say once that respecting your beliefs sometimes means giving up things you really want.*

And right now she was making the biggest sacrifice she'd ever made. But would she be able to do it? *I have to. There's no other option.* Her shoulders slumped. She lowered her chin a notch.

God sent His only son to die on the cross for our sins. When compared to that great sacrifice, what she had to do seemed simple. Yet why was it so difficult?

She shrugged. A lone tear slid down her cheek.

Stopping her feelings for Levi wouldn't be easy. The truth was, she didn't know if it was possible. The more she tried to solve her dilemma, the clearer reality became.

Finally, as she decided what she needed to do, Annie also realized why she had such trouble with it.

The issue wasn't about her. It wasn't about Levi either. The whole crux of the problem had to do with what he did to her heart. She wanted to spend her life with one man. And that very individual was the one person off-limits to her.

Chapter Eight

The following morning, a bright ray of sunlight made its way in through the opened two-story window of Old Sam's barn. A cool breeze coming in pushed a couple of blond hairs out of place. Taking a careful finger, Annie placed them back under her *kapp*. Ginger whinnied and snorted.

Annie knew the signals by heart. So did Sam. Grinning, Annie rose from the wooden rocker he had made especially for her and stepped to Ginger, running an affectionate hand over her thick brown mane. "You need attention, don't you?"

In response, the horse wagged her long neck and clomped an impatient hoof against the cement. Annie reassured the old gal she loved her. After planting a firm kiss on the dirt-brown face that smelled of straw, Annie returned to her spot.

Stepping closer to the artist and his project, she took in Old Sam's passionate expression as he bent over a beautiful oak board and etched lines into wood with great care and detail. Others had attempted to match his uncanny ability to create the very designs that made his work come alive.

Annie remembered what she'd told Levi about something bad turning into something good. Esther's passing had resulted in Annie's close friendship with the hope chest designer and his unique talent. She studied the widower's face and pressed her lips together thoughtfully. It was the poster visage of wisdom and insightfulness. He'd once told her that every line on his skin represented a lesson in life.

She trusted Sam to keep what she said in confidence. And she was certain he wouldn't judge her. She wanted to talk to him about Levi. She couldn't go to Mamma. And definitely not to Elizabeth. To talk to them would send out unnecessary alarms and cause more worry. Her journal, unfortunately, didn't offer desperately needed answers.

She cleared the knot in her throat. "Sam, there's something I want to ask you."

He stopped to raise an inquisitive brow. The lines around his eyes deepened. "By the serious tone in your voice, I'm guessing it's something important."

She drew in a small sigh. "Uh-huh."

He blew on the chest lid. Dust particles floated gracefully in the air before settling on the floor. In the background a pair of pigeons fluttered their wings.

"It's about Levi Miller and me."

It was his last night in Arthur. Levi stared out of the bedroom window. Lightning crackled. As he contemplated his day with Annie, he pressed his lips together in deep thought. Emotions hit him from all directions as he recalled details of their time together. Would he ever see her again? Would he come back someday to be with little Jake?

He gave a slow, sad shake of his head, absorbing every detail about his uncle's place to store it in his repertoire. The second-story window overlooking the pasture. The gas tanks next to the barn. The black family buggy parked underneath the side extension of the house. The family well.

In the distance, Pebble Creek loomed. Because of the storm, Levi couldn't see its mouth. But he could imagine it and smiled. Before the rain had started, he'd watched forty-odd cattle make their way in queues into his uncle's exceptionally large red barn. He closed his eyes for a moment to enjoy the vivid memories that flooded his mind. He pictured the inside of the old barn, which he knew like the back of his hand. He'd spent a lot of time in there, lifting heavy bales of hay. He recalled the long silver feeding trough. Excess hay bales stacked to the ceiling. He knew well where the family horse was quartered and the wall that separated it from the cattle. Aluminum milking pails. Extra feed. The dried ears of corn he and Jake had fed the squirrels.

He drifted back over ten years. Mornings and afternoons spent working in the yard had been happy times. He by no means regretted growing up Amish. In fact, as he contemplated the entire picture, he came up with many reasons to respect and admire the Plain Faith. At times, he even missed it. He had loved going to school with Annie. The singings.

He'd never forget the delicious homemade food. It wasn't as if he didn't eat well now, but since he'd become English, he'd missed dishes made from scratch. He admitted there was no comparison between the pies at the wedding and the store-bought ones they ate at home. Packaged noodles couldn't hold a candle to the ones his mom used to make. And Amish soup could beat out any in the English world hands down.

Right after their move, his mother had cooked as she always had. However, as time went on, she'd come to play an ever larger role in his dad's quickly growing business. Not only did she keep the books but she ordered materials and checked them off as they came in. He didn't expect her to bake like she used to; there wasn't time. Their freezer was filled with instant dinners. Levi didn't mind, but boy, did he enjoy his aunt's home-cooked meals.

As he watched, the rain beating on the roof became more intense. Puddles already had formed in the dirt space between the barn and the old shed. Thunder was now a continuous rumble. Lightning bolts brightened the sky without pause.

Levi stepped closer to the window for one last glimpse of Pebble Creek. Although the vision was little more than a blur, he drew in a deep, emotional sigh. He knew what it looked like by heart. The creek wound its way through the vacant plot owned by Old Sam. Pebbles at the bottom made the narrow body of water clear; the deepest part was a couple of feet.

Levi loved how the stream made its lazy way from the mouth, up part of the hill, and back down to the end, where it narrowed and eventually stopped. Tall patches of dead weeds put an end to the flow. The land pulled at his heartstrings. Or was that Annie? Was it possible to separate the two?

He gave a slow shake of his head. The beautiful land owned by Old Sam had been passed down to him by his great grandparents. To Levi's knowledge, Sam didn't intend to sell it; the elderly man enjoyed taking Buddy for walks along the stream. Although Old Sam owned the coveted property, Levi still considered it his and Annie's. The place had played as large a role in the first ten years of Levi's life as milking cows. Baling hay. Building houses.

An unusual sense of calm swept through him as he recalled the times he and Annie had walked the entire length of the property. In the middle, they had bridged their own crossing to make it to the other side.

Levi's brief visit here had given him much-needed closure for the early part of his life. Seeing people from his youth had been like going on a pleasant journey back in time. Some good had come from his time here, had provided him some peace of mind.

He clasped his hands together until his knuckles popped. He tapped the toe of his shoe nervously against the hardwood floor. He was finally home. But he couldn't live here. He tried to make sense of this awkward situation. How could your home be a place you couldn't live?

He slid his hands down far into the deep pockets of his blue jeans and rested his thumbs over the thick seams. He threw his head back in frustration. He closed his eyes for a moment and Annie's beautiful face popped into his mind. He took a deep breath to gather his composure.

Their childhood had been ripped apart. Yet ten years later, they had immediately picked up where they'd left off, as if they'd never been separated. This time, leaving her would be different from before. He planned to stay in touch. *I want more.* For some reason, he needed her like he needed air. Their friendship was strong. In a strange way, it was as if she was part of him. Perhaps it was because they knew each other so well. He could write her. Call the phone shanty her family shared with the neighbors, too, though he didn't want to cause a stir in her community.

It didn't take much to start talk. He wouldn't cause her pain. In the Amish world, Annie didn't have many choices. In the Plain Faith, men and women had set roles. If gossip started about him and Annie, she'd never be able to escape the community's wrath. He wouldn't be here to endure it, but she would. He needed to protect her. To do that, he must end their happy relationship.

A strong bolt of lightning stopped his thoughts. The cracking sound was so loud, he jumped. In a split second, bright orange flames sprang from the barn's roof. He blinked to make sure he hadn't imagined the fire.

Catching a surprised breath, he ran out into the hall and shouted, "Uncle Marlin! The barn's on fire!" Levi's heart pumped like a runner's at the finish line, and he bolted down the stairs.

Jake ran barefoot to the door. Uncle Marlin and Aunt Abigail were putting on their shoes. Levi's emergency training kicked in. He hollered, "Call for help! I'll start putting out the fire!"

His uncle rushed out of the house to the phone shanty. At the same time, the cattle were causing a commotion escaping the barn and migrating to the far side of the pasture, mooing frantically.

Levi ran to the well, connected the hose from the nearby shed, and dragged it to the base of the barn. But the size of the fire immediately told him it wouldn't be nearly enough. He prayed for help to come quickly. Because fire moved fast. And a blaze of this magnitude could easily spread to the house and shed in no time at all. He was fully aware that there were flammable liquids inside the barn.

He heard the siren. The moment the bright red truck pulled up, he motioned toward the blaze. "Lightning struck. Flammable liquids inside."

His uncle and the neighbors who'd shown up already were fighting the wicked fire with well water. Unfortunately, the rain had become nothing more than a light sprinkle. Levi wished it would pour again to help extinguish the flames.

The blaze was so bright, Levi forgot it was nighttime. The cows' loud protests echoed through the cool, wet air in the pasture. The sharp sound of glass breaking prompted Levi to look up. He wasn't wearing protective gear. It wasn't long before gray smoke filled the air. The heavy, deadly clouds made it difficult to see.

Firemen made their way up two ladders and aimed their yellow attack lines at the base of the fire. Spectators gathered. Levi shouted, "Stay back!" He motioned with strong hands. "Keep away!" His lungs struggled to pump air. It was difficult to breathe without compressed air over his face, but he would do whatever he could to stop the fire from taking little Jake's house.

Despite the working crew that had assembled in a matter of minutes, the blaze continued to grow. A huge sense of urgency filled Levi's soul as he climbed to the top of a ladder, helping to carry a heavy hose. Water oozed onto the flames, but the fire wouldn't die. He retraced his steps back down to the ground for an additional hose. For one blissful moment, the flames disappeared. At the same time, the spectators breathed in. An eerie silence loomed. The only sound was of water spraying. But Levi doubted the threat was over. Experience had taught him to expect a rebound fire.

Before he could start back up the ladder, an explosion broke the silence and smoke oozed in dark clouds. Screams filled the air as the crew continued spraying. Levi's eyes burned. The heat was so intense, he looked down to make sure he hadn't caught fire himself. His lungs pumped hard, and it was becoming almost impossible to breathe. Time seemed to stand still as he struggled. Finally, Levi sighed in relief when the orange monster began to succumb. He and the other volunteers continued to douse the flames.

Even though a sense of relief and calm had set in, Levi still worried that the fire would reignite. Fighting a blaze involving flammable liquids was a tricky, unpredictable job. Deadly smoke now filled his lungs until he started to feel light-headed.

As he stepped away for air, a nauseating odor

surrounded him. Everyone watched as wooden slabs broke free from the barn. Boards dropped from the structure, reminding Levi of a slingshot he'd had as a kid. In seconds, the rest of the building came undone. The worst nightmare had come true. Everything inside of the barn was being destroyed. Hundreds of bales of hay for the livestock. Oats. Barley. Tools. Ladders. Gasoline and kerosene.

The all-too-familiar, sickening odor of death made Levi's stomach churn. The knot in his throat nearly choked him, but he swallowed it and squared his shoulders.

He glimpsed Jake running toward him as a sudden, enormous crack prompted everyone to look up. A huge piece of the barn flew like an arrow in the direction of the little boy. In a heartbeat, Levi jumped toward Jake, shoved him out of the way, and took the hit on the back of his head. His world went black.

Levi blinked. Hushed voices whispered nearby. He couldn't make out the words, but he didn't really care. Not sure where he was, Levi opened his eyes.

This time he noticed his uncle and aunt standing next to him. He was on his back with his head propped up on pillows. A plastic tube dangled from his arm. Uncle Marlin looked Levi in the eye. His eyes reflected a combination of worry and relief. "Son, you're in the hospital."

The statement sank in as Levi took in his feet

sticking out of white cotton covers. The room was sparse, with two chairs and medical paraphernalia.

Levi raised his free hand to touch the bandage on the side of his neck. "Ouch."

A nurse stepped into the room and gently pulled his fingers away. Her voice was soft yet firm as she shook her head. "Try not to touch it. The cut's pretty bad. Any deeper and you wouldn't be here right now. You're lucky to be alive. God was watching out for you."

He tried to stay awake so he could figure out what she meant. His eyes closed, and when he opened them again, the three people in the room gazed at him with uncertainty.

He wanted to speak, but agonizing pain in his neck stopped him. Finally, words came out in a barely audible tone. "What happened?" He coughed. It felt like something was stuck in his throat.

The nurse patted his arm as if he were a child. Then she put her finger to her lips. "Shh. Don't say anything. Just rest and know that Dr. Morris is confident you're going to be fine."

Levi tried to verbalize the questions that flitted through his mind, but he couldn't process his thoughts. His uncle's words came in a very low, emotional tone: "The barn burned. There's nothing left."

Several moments later, the statement sank in. Levi gave a slow nod of recognition.

"The siding snapped off; a big piece flew toward little Jake, but you jumped in front of him to save his life." There was a long hesitation as Uncle Marlin caught an emotional breath. When he continued, his voice cracked. "It would have killed him, Levi. It nearly got you." His uncle wrapped his arm around his wife and they both hugged and cried.

The news slowly sank in until Levi finally recognized what they were talking about. *Lightning. Fire.*

When they finally regained their composure, Uncle Marlin touched Levi's arm with gentleness and love. "Your folks are on their way. Levi, you're a hero. We're indebted to you. How can we ever repay you?"

His words stopped while they wept again. As Levi tried to digest what he'd just said, his head pounded with great ferocity. He closed his eyes and commanded the terrible pain to stop. He was still struggling to remember what had happened. In what seemed to be a dream, he could see the barn burst into flames in vivid detail. Fire suddenly erupted where the bolt of lightning struck. He'd called for help. The building had come apart with foggy gray smoke. Difficulty breathing. Volunteers fighting the fire. Firemen.

Levi's heart picked up to an antagonizing speed as he envisioned uncontrollable boards flying off the building like slingshots. But he had no recollection of stepping in front of little Jake. Frustrated, Levi squeezed his eyes closed and struggled to recall the action that had spared his cousin's life.

The sound of footsteps prompted him to open his eyes and look at the door. A nurse entered the room with a syringe between her fingers. While she spoke, she injected something into Levi's IV. He was out.

* * *

Later, Levi continued to try to recall the moment that had landed him in the hospital. A man—Dr. Morris?—knocked on the door and entered the room before Levi could open his eyes. When he did, he was surprised and happy to see his folks at his bedside.

The physician touched Levi's hand in reassurance. "You look better. You gave us all a scare." While he checked the papers in his hand, Levi tried to smile at his parents.

The expression in his mother's hazel eyes was a combination of relief and devastation. Her hair was cut shorter than usual. With great care not to disturb his tubes, she bent to kiss his cheek. Gently running her fingers through his hair, she whispered, "Sweetheart, you're going to be okay." The moment those words were spoken, her eyes flooded with moisture.

Automatically, Levi's gaze shifted to the deep concern on his dad's face. The unreadable expression brought unexpected emotion to Levi's throat. He tried to swallow the thickness there.

Dr. Morris broke the silence. "Tomorrow we'll take him off the oxygen." He turned back to Levi. "How's the headache?"

If Levi could have managed a laugh without pain, he would have let one out. But he found he couldn't even smile without causing a fierce pounding in his head. He yearned to chuckle at the way the doctor had said *headache.* The agony in his head was hardly that. It felt more like an entire block of concrete had been dropped on top of him.

When he realized the doctor expected a response, he focused. Levi took pride in being strong. No matter how much he hurt, he didn't complain. His parents were already worried; he needed to convince them he was all right. "I'm okay."

The doctor's smile was a combination of doubt and satisfaction. "That's music to my ears. We've got as much Toradol in your IV as we can give you to curb the pain. There's no magic bullet to get you out of here, son. We'll just have to be patient and let the healing process begin. I'll check in later to see how you're doing."

When the doctor turned to leave, Levi lifted a hand to stop him. Words came out of his mouth, though he could barely hear them. Thankfully, Dr. Morris leaned closer. "Doctor, I don't remember pushing my cousin out of the way. I try . . ." He closed his heavy lids in agony. "The last thing I remember seeing is the board flying off the barn."

Dr. Morris nodded in understanding and pressed his lips together, as if trying for the best response. "You suffered a severe concussion. I've dealt with numerous trauma victims in the past; unfortunately, I can't predict what will happen because there's no clear-cut pattern for head injuries. Everyone reacts differently. But . . ." He ran his hand over the top of his head. "There's no rushing the brain, but I think it's safe to say that most of my patients eventually regain full memory. I can't promise if or when you'll have full recollection of what happened. All I can suggest is to focus on getting plenty of rest and in time, hopefully, you'll have full recall."

Levi gave a slow nod of understanding as his eyes closed again. His last thought before he dozed off was of Annie.

Chapter Nine

The moment Levi awakened, he thought he was in heaven. An unusual expression that was a combination of relief and worry filled Annie's eyes. Her creamy complexion looked so perfect, it was difficult to believe she didn't use makeup. As usual, her thick mass of hair was tucked neatly under her *kapp.*

She smiled. "Don't talk," she ordered in a sympathetic tone. "The doctor said the laceration on your neck took twenty-one stitches. They'll take a while to heal, you know."

"Stitches?"

She nodded. "That panel hit you so hard, it could have killed you. And little Jake . . ." Annie drew her hands up to her chest and she breathed in a deep sigh of appreciation. "He's alive because of you." She wiggled her hands in the air. "Everyone's talking about it. And your parents . . ." She sighed and strummed her fingers against the metal bed rail. "They just left to get something to eat."

He remembered seeing them. His uncle must have

contacted them about the accident. Unfortunately, even though something as devastating as his accident should bring the family closer together, he knew the shunning would continue forever. He agreed with Annie about liking happy endings.

Levi squinted as a ray of sunshine slipped into the dull-looking room.

"I'll close the blinds."

Before Annie could move, he reached out and squeezed her hand to stop her.

She frowned. "You want them open?"

He nodded.

Levi glimpsed the clock on the wall. Then the window. The blinds were open and the sun was high in the sky. He wondered how long he'd been asleep but didn't think too long because of the fierce pounding in his temples.

Annie's voice was soft and understanding. It was as comforting as a blanket must be to a newborn. "Are you . . . better?"

He considered the question and finally moved his head a little. He wasn't great; that was for certain. However, the pain had subsided a little.

She squeezed his hand with strong affection. "*Gut.* The doctor says you'll be just fine." She eyed the chair in the corner. "I brought you some snacks," she said, motioning to a small basket.

The corners of his lips lifted a little. To his delight, he felt well enough to tease her. "Sponge cakes?"

She laid a gentle hand on his arm. "You really shouldn't try to talk much. *Jah.* Sponge cakes." She put her other hand on his. "And other treats, too."

She paused. "It will be nice when you're better. But there's plenty of time to talk about that. Right now, just rest. You've been through a lot."

He nodded and wondered why his throat hurt so much if it was his neck that was injured.

As if reading his mind, Annie went on. "The nurse said you breathed in a lot of smoke. Not only that but the siding hit you pretty bad."

She caressed his fingers in a gentle, reassuring manner. She didn't worry about breaking a rule. There was no way she could look at him like this and not touch him. Her voice cracked when she spoke. "Levi, I can't believe this happened. If only you'd left before the fire . . ."

"We would have lost little Jake."

Tears filled her eyes and she quickly looked away. "I wish I could have helped."

His heart nearly melted.

"I'm so glad you're alive!"

Levi closed his eyes while she tightened her grip on his hand. In a silent prayer, he thanked the Lord for Annie. For helping him to save little Jake. And for being alive. He couldn't begin to imagine the devastation such a huge loss would cause their family. An ache pinched his chest, and he immediately blocked that awful thought from his mind.

The reassuring warmth of Annie's fingers penetrated his own and miraculously made its way through his entire body, settling in his toes. For long blissful moments, he enjoyed the comforting sensation. Perhaps this would heal him faster than the medicine in the IV.

The throbbing in his head subsided for a few

moments and he opened his eyes. Breathing a sigh of relief, Annie returned his warm gesture. While he studied her face, he marveled at her lovely features. Of course everything about her was already etched into his mind. But right now, as he studied her intently, he appreciated what was right in front of him even more. Her girlish grin had turned into a killer smile. She was totally unaware of her innocent allure. He silently chastised himself for finding her so attractive. In the Amish faith, they didn't focus on outer beauty but rather what lay inside. Of course he wasn't Amish.

Obviously Annie had both. And the boys his age within the community? He was sure they must notice her knockout appearance. After all, they were human. And they weren't blind. They just knew better than to voice their opinions. But Annie's strongest point, in his opinion, wasn't what was on the outside. It was rare for an individual to possess such a nurturing quality. And such kindness and sincerity. She would make a good nurse.

Even as he lay there in his narrow hospital bed, just looking at the sincerity in her eyes and listening to the compassion in her voice made him feel better than the Toradol ever could.

Annie continued to hold his hand as he closed his eyes and drifted back to over a decade before, when they'd tossed pebbles into the clear, shallow water of the creek.

He remembered when he had gotten a splinter in his hand while helping his dad build a house for two newlyweds. At the time, Annie had been inside with the young wife, putting dishes away. She had been

quick to attend to his injury, kindly ordering him to hold still while she removed with great care the small piece of wood with a pair of tweezers. She was meticulous. She had finished the job by applying peroxide to the injured area.

Then he recalled another occasion when he'd been at school with a head cold. The following day, Annie had brought vitamin C and a tea bag in her lunch pail. She had made him a cup of the hot drink with her own herbs. He wondered if she still grew them.

He pressed his lips together thoughtfully and mentally compared her to English girls. Levi had admitted to her that he wasn't fond of the Amish faith. And for good reason. After all, how could he justify a religion that had ousted someone just because he broke one rule. At the same time, that very faith had made Annie who she was. And for that he was truly thankful. He respected her for her strength. She had always been loyal to her beliefs. To the *Ordnung*. And he commended her for it. Because being in her shoes wasn't easy. Before the shunning, Levi had never realized the toughness the Plain Faith required. Like hitching a horse to a buggy when he needed a ride. Now, all he did was step into his car and turn the ignition.

Levi began to relax and closed his eyes. There was one thing that stayed with him as he drifted off to sleep. Something Uncle Marlin had said. That they were indebted to him, and if there was anything they could do . . .

* * *

The gas heater was on, but Annie's bedroom was on the cool side. Even though it was only the last part of October, it felt like December as she stretched her hands above her head and stood on tiptoe to let out a long, happy sigh. Levi was going to be okay.

Thankfully, God had protected everyone from the devastating fire. She was sure her Savior had brought Levi back to the wedding to save little Jake. Now, that was clear.

The pleasant smell of homemade butter filled the house. Annie closed her eyes for a moment to enjoy the comforting aroma. Something about Mamma's cooking always made her feel protected and loved.

She went to her precious hope chest, opened the beautiful lid, and retrieved her journal. She left the lid up to admire the deep blue velvet lining while she found a comfortable spot on the floor.

As she glanced around the four corners of the polished hardwood floor, she adjusted the rug under her hips. Sitting against the bed, she bent her legs at the knees and rested the journal on her thighs. With great care, she opened the small book to an empty page and dated the top right corner.

Emotions floated through her heart in every direction. The best way to figure them out was to put pen to paper. It was the only method she knew of to get her priorities in order.

Today I got happy news that Levi will be fine. That he should be released in a couple of days.

She paused to look up at the bright moonbeam slipping into the room. Then she bent her head and focused on her thoughts. Finally, she put her pen back to the page in front of her.

It's devastating that the Millers' barn burned down. The Lord must have brought Levi back to protect little Jake. I'm so thankful He looked after Levi, too. It's difficult to imagine the Miller family starting over . . . It's late in the year to rebuild a barn of that size. In fact, it might not be finished before spring.

She frowned at the negative thought. She always focused on the positive. So she mentally ordered her glass to be half full, not half empty. And sighed her relief. Her shoulders relaxed.

Looking on the up side, perhaps this will be a new beginning in more ways than one?

She paused to substantiate her statement.

This particular incident will surely bind Levi closer to his cousins, aunt, and uncle. God temporarily kept Levi here. His heart aches to be close to his family again. He's never said it in so many words, but I feel as if I can read his mind. It's got to be the reason he returned.

She gave a sad shake of her head.

I can't imagine how Levi and his parents felt when they left. But I understand why he's disappointed with our faith. We let him down. But what's happened is, in a way, a miracle. I'm not sure what will become of this, but I will pray that Levi's act of bravery will somehow pull his whole family together.

For long moments she pressed her lips together and tensed as she realized the significance of what she'd just admitted on the lines in front of her.

She looked up at the moon and wondered if she should erase her last thoughts. But wasn't the point of a journal to express your innermost feelings? If she didn't write what she felt, what good was a journal? And no one would ever read it but her. First of all, it was an unwritten rule not to look at someone else's journal, wasn't it?

Deciding to move forward with her sentiment, she put her pen to paper again and pushed out a determined, honest breath.

I believe God's love is all about forgiveness. My community is like an extended family. If we don't forgive others, wouldn't God be disappointed?

Her hand stiffened with uneasiness as she translated the feelings in her heart into words.

I still don't agree that we should have shunned Levi's dad. If he had killed someone . . . if he had abused . . . it would be different.

She frowned and swallowed the knot in her throat.

But that wasn't the case. Yes, when John Miller drove his own truck, he broke a rule he'd committed to when he joined the church. But the way I understand it, he was put in a pinch when his driver quit.

Standing, she put her journal and pen aside on the floor. She paced the room a couple of times before reclaiming her spot.

She looked back at her written thoughts and assessed them. Before continuing, she questioned her beliefs. Her parents would surely be disappointed that she disagreed with the harsh punishment for breaking the rules.

She returned her journal to Old Sam's beautiful gift. As the light, pleasant scent of oak filled her nostrils, she smiled. The smell prompted comfort. She closed the lid with great care and focused on the recipe. She traced her finger over the ingredients that Sam had engraved with such expertise.

She blinked at the sudden sting of tears. While her hand lingered on Sam's work, she allowed her mind to wander. Something about this sentimental piece pulled her to it every evening. It had become a significant part of her life. Because buried inside lay her innermost thoughts. Things she didn't dare share with anyone, not even Old Sam. Written between the lines were her greatest fears. Her strongest loves. Her secret dreams.

For a blissful moment, she closed her eyes and dared to imagine a future with the man she'd loved her entire life. She even envisioned them with children. In her own home, the very house Levi built especially for her. At Pebble Creek.

She imagined manicuring the front yard hedge and planting tiny petunia plants in front.

Before getting into bed, Annie knelt beside the oversize comforter and squeezed her eyes closed. She pressed her palms together and quietly said the Lord's Prayer.

"Dear God, You know me better than I know myself. I pray with all my heart that John Miller will be welcomed back with open arms, just like he's one of us, and that everyone will forget the past and concentrate on what's ahead. Please bless my wonderful parents and family. And I thank You for bringing Levi back to me. Lord, I know it looks impossible for us to be together." She inhaled a shaky breath and pressed her hands together as hard as she could. "But You work miracles. God, I want to remain in the Amish faith. I also long to grow old with Levi. My dream is to be his wife. Please, Lord. Let that happen. Amen."

At Pebble Creek, the late October sun warmed Annie's face. Levi's hands were deep in his pockets, his back to Annie, and he appeared to gaze at the shallow body of water that was unique and special to both of them.

As she stepped closer, she shouted and offered a friendly wave. "Hello!"

He returned the gesture with a big smile and made his way toward her. When they met, he motioned her to the path that paralleled the creek. That dirt walk had become their very own.

"You look better every day!"

"I'm glad I have my folks' blessing to stay here to finish my doctor visits. I've had exceptional care. And I really wanted to contribute to the new barn."

"Mamma always told me that recovery's fifty percent attitude."

"Enough about me. How are you?"

"I went to Sam's with a special delivery."

Levi's grin was mischievous. "Like I've said . . ."

She chimed in. "I know; I know. He's one spoiled man." She glanced in the direction of the Miller house. "How's your uncle's barn coming?"

"Fast; it's gonna be better than ever. Soon Uncle Marlin will get his cattle back from the neighbors. Then he'll be back in business."

The reality of his admission quickly set in. *Levi will be going home. I prepared myself for it once. Now I'll have to do it again. This time I know it will happen. And I dread it.*

A large, hard knot caught in her throat. She tried not to cough; instead, she attempted to disguise her concern by lifting the pitch of her voice. "I'm glad things are back to normal."

"It's nice the way everyone pitched in. You know, when folks got wind that there was no insurance, total strangers became good Samaritans. Between them and the money from this community, everything can get done."

She nodded, and they walked in silence. Every once in a while, Levi bent to pick up a pebble and throw it into the stream. Each time, both he and Annie smiled when the water splashed. Then, they continued on. The cool breeze blew a few loose hairs from under her *kapp*; Annie didn't bother to tuck them back under her covering where they belonged. Levi was leaving for good. The rest of her life would be devoid of the man she loved with all her heart. What did it matter if a few strands of hair fell over her cheeks?

For long moments they gazed at each other. The flecks in his eyes danced with an unusual flare. "You want to sit down?"

"Sure."

When they reached their spot on top of the hill, he motioned for her to sit. When she did so, he knelt to join her. Whenever she was close to Levi, she felt secure. Like the earth could rumble but she would still be okay. With Levi, she felt she could do anything. There were no restrictions on their potential. Next to him, she had no fears. Only happiness. Contentment. She'd never experienced such a wonderful, calming sensation with anyone in her life.

They both stared down at the clover patch between their shoes. With one very slow motion, Levi bent to pluck a clover from the ground. When he sat up, he eyed the plant between his two fingers.

She glimpsed it and immediately noticed it had an extra leaf. When Levi lifted his eyes, they both smiled. "A four-leaf clover," he said. "There aren't many of these around." The expression in his eyes was proud. "Maybe one out of ten thousand or so?" There was excitement in his voice. "I'm sure you've heard the story about it bringing good luck."

She nodded. "The English even have a special day for it, don't they?"

"Yeah, but there's more to it than good fortune.

Mom once told me an interesting story about how it relates to Christianity."

She crossed her legs at the ankles and rested her palms against the hard ground. "I'd like to hear it."

With the pointer finger of his left hand, he touched each small leaf, one by one. "Three leaves supposedly stand for the Father, the Son, and the Holy Ghost." He paused and eyed her with a certain seriousness. "But the fourth represents the grace of God. Some even say the four leaves resemble a cross."

"That's a beautiful story." She smiled. "Thanks for sharing it."

He raised a mischievous brow and continued. "There's another old saga about the four-leaf clover that started long before St. Patrick's Day." He gave a careless shrug of his shoulders and grinned. "It's probably nothing but a good story, but it goes that Eve took a four-leaf clover with her when she left the Garden of Eden." He lowered his voice to a more confidential, serious tone and she leaned forward so she could hear better. "And you know what that means, don't you?"

She listened with intent interest. For an Amish girl, she was quite sure she had way too much imagination.

"That means, Annie, that anyone lucky enough to find it will get a taste of paradise."

The corners of her lips pulled upward into a satisfied smile. "That's better than the best of Old Sam's stories. Of course we'll never know if it's true."

He gave an amused roll of his eyes. "Maybe not, but don't you wonder?"

She giggled. It was the combination of the acute interest in his voice and the way he rolled his eyes that made her laugh. "We'll never know."

"Myths are interesting."

She sat up straight and uncrossed her legs to bend them. She adjusted her position and wrapped her arms around her knees to hold them in place. The wind picked up a bit, and she pulled at the front of her coat for more warmth.

Levi continued to eye the clover as if it was a special find. A prize. And it was . . . if all the stories surrounding it were true.

"I know with all my heart that real miracles happen." She looked at the stream in the distance. The hill on which they sat. "Only God can make a miracle. But it's up to us to ask Him for it. And sometimes . . ." She took a breath. "It takes longer than we'd like. But there must be a reason; we just don't know it. In the end, God rewards the faithful."

A long, happy silence ensued before he nodded. "I like that. And I'm sure what you say is true. In other words, there's a happy ending to every story. If we pray and have faith."

She responded with a slow nod of confirmation while she considered her own words. She truly believed them. Did Levi, too? She studied his expression, which was an odd combination of hope and doubt. She wasn't sure of Levi's every thought, but she did know him unusually well. Even though they'd missed a decade together, she knew his heart. It would never change. And she guessed Levi wanted more than anything to dissolve his father's shunning. Maybe he wished his dad could get another chance with the faith. With all her heart, that was what Annie wanted.

But it was up to John Miller to make that happen. And from what she knew, Levi's dad had never repented. John had never even apologized; nor had he tried to stay in their faith. So what happened was out of her control. Levi's too.

At the same time, Levi's interesting stories had sparked her interest. She couldn't stop thinking about Eve leaving the Garden of Eden with a four-leaf clover in her hand.

Something else wouldn't leave Annie alone, too. Her strong belief that God would carve out a plan for Annie to be with Levi. She had no idea how He would make it happen. She was fully aware that her wish was a high hope and unlikely to materialize. And observing the situation between the families and faiths, the outcome of a union between her and Levi appeared impossible. But God worked miracles. That she was sure of.

Levi leaned closer and handed her his special find. She held out a steady hand, ready to place the other palm over it so the wind wouldn't blow it away. "For you, Annie. Maybe you can preserve it to remind you of our time at Pebble Creek."

As she took the small, faded plant between her fingers, the light sensation from his touch created an amazing sort of reassurance. A comforting sensation. As if God had gifted them a special blessing to bond them even tighter.

She looked around, wondering where to put the clover while they finished their conversation. If she put it on the rock, the wind would take it. If she stuck it in her pocket, it might tear or slip out. She considered the best place to keep it and smiled in satisfaction.

"What are you thinking?" His tone was curious.

"I never want to forget your interesting stories about the clover; the attention we've already given it makes it truly special, so I'll take it home to press and keep it in my hope chest."

"You want me to stick it in my pocket?"

She eyed his denim and gave a shake of her head. "It's too fragile." She eyed the plant before meeting his gaze. "Will you help me put it under my *kapp*?"

A doubtful expression crossed his face. "Are you sure?"

"*Jah*. It will be safe there. At least until I get home."

"Okay." As she removed a pin from her hair, she carefully placed the clover underneath the soft ends. He held down her *kapp* while she tucked it under the pin.

Moments later, the wind died down and they reclaimed their original seats on the large stones. She sensed an uncertainty in his demeanor from the way he fidgeted with his hands. He kept wringing them together; finally, he decided on a place to rest them. On his thighs. What on earth was wrong? Was he sick?

"Levi . . ."

When he spoke his voice was firm but emotional. "I'm okay. Just a little . . . nervous."

"About what?"

He faced her. When she'd glimpsed his fingers, she'd noticed they were shaking. Their faces were so close, her nose nearly touching his. His warm breath fanned her eyelashes.

"Annie, we've always been honest with each other."

To her surprise, his voice suddenly sounded soft and uncertain. What on earth was he about to tell her? Her heart picked up speed until it raced with uncertainty. "*Jah*."

"I'm going through something that . . ." He pressed his lips together. "It's difficult."

"I know."

Surprise flickered in his eyes. "You do?"

She offered a slow nod and found her most sympathetic voice. "I think so."

"Have you been wondering about us?"

Their eyes locked and she didn't let her gaze leave his. Again, she offered a slow, brave nod.

He squared his shoulders, as if defending himself. To her astonishment, he stood and paced in front of her. "I like to know exactly what to do. I don't feel comfortable when I'm not in control. In charge." He hesitated. "So, Annie, I've been trying to figure something out." He stopped in front of her and looked down. His voice cracked with emotion. "About you. Even though we're different faiths, we're still . . . the same."

She sat unusually still, trying to understand what he was trying to convey. The wind disappeared. Geese flew south in a V shape.

His voice had lowered to a pitch that was barely more than a whisper. He knelt and breathed. "Annie, I love you. I've tried to stop, but I can't."

As she took in his words, her heart nearly stopped with happiness and shock. It was pumping so hard, she was afraid it would jump out of her chest. She closed her eyes for a moment to say a silent prayer of thanks. When she opened them, they both stood. This was a dream come true. Maybe there was truth to the clover story.

She spoke from her heart. "Oh, Levi. I love you, too. I mean, I think I always did, but now it's different." She paused for a moment to take a deep, brave breath. "I want you to stay. Forever."

He gazed down at her. She'd never seen such intensity in his eyes. The flecks were going crazy.

"I know our situation isn't ideal. But do you think we could make this work?"

Excitement edged his voice. "Just think, Annie; you could move away with me. We could get married, have children, and I would build you the beautiful home you've always wanted. I promise to take good care of you. Better than anyone in the world." His voice cracked with emotion. "I want to grow old with you."

Tears that were a combination of great joy and sadness slipped down her cheeks. At the same time, clouds covered the sun, and a sudden chill prompted shivers up Annie's arms. But she didn't try to warm herself. Her heart flooded with love for this man who had told her he wanted to spend his life with her.

Now wasn't the time to be shy. She used her most direct tone. "What about joining the Amish church? Is that what we would do?"

The corners of his mouth drooped. Her heart sank. The dismayed expression on his face told her everything. She almost cried as she leaned forward. "Levi? Please. Come back. It's where you belong."

Levi dropped her hands and walked away. Annie shivered. Her heart pumped to an uncertain beat as she watched him. When he came back to her, she looked at him for an answer.

His eyes filled with a combination of hope and disappointment. "Annie, you said yourself that God works miracles. Right now, I have faith that we'll be together. Forever."

Her pulse sprinted with great anticipation. "I want that, too."

They headed to the creek. The small creek had a way of creating happiness. It was a silent bond between them. And now they had a four-leaf clover . . .

While shallow water floated over pebbles, Levi shook his head. Color drained from his cheeks. The warmth from his fingers turned as cold as ice cubes. "Annie, I can't come back."

"Of course you can. You're loved here, Levi. What about . . ."

He stopped her with a firm, decisive tone. "I don't deny that I miss things about the Plain Faith. Being here has reminded me just how engrained this life is in my heart. I can live without electricity, although I would miss certain things, like cold air when it's hot in the summer. And driving my own truck. Especially with our business."

"It's good to know you've missed the community. Levi, it's not a perfect world. But we have to make this work." She added in a softer, more desperate voice, "Because I can't live without you."

He hugged her. She wanted to stay in his embrace

forever. Where nothing could harm her. Where her dreams came alive. Right now she needed her Savior more than ever. Only by His grace and love could her situation with Levi be worked out. She said a silent prayer for help.

When he held her at arm's length, he gave a hopeful sigh. "I've been trying to think of a way, Annie. And here's what I decided. We could join the Mennonite church. And we'd live pretty much the way you're used to . . ."

She frowned. "But they use electricity."

"Yup, but it's still pretty similar to the Amish. Annie, I can't come back to my roots." He gave a frustrated roll of his eyes. "And you can't expect me to. My family's been through too much. You know that."

"Levi, they never shunned you."

"But it's the same thing, Annie. My family relocated and started over. If I did come back and joined the church, I'd always be regarded as the son of a shunned man."

She lowered her gaze to her black shoes. She didn't know what to say. Because she agreed that shunning was harsh punishment for something that hadn't really harmed anyone. She tried for the right words. "Levi, the reason for shunning is to make a person repent for what he did. I'm sure the bishop wanted your dad to apologize; if he had, he would have been welcomed back with open arms."

A long, tense silence ensued. "Do you really believe that, Annie? You think this town would have just forgotten that he'd driven his truck?"

She regarded him in silence. She couldn't say.

Because, honestly, she wasn't sure. In her heart, she wouldn't have been able to shun John Miller. Instead, she would have reached out to help him. She supposed no faith was perfect, and hers wasn't an exception. She spoke in a regretful tone. "You know my thoughts."

"Then you'll join the Mennonite church with me, Annie?" He paused to clear his throat. "At least think about it?"

All of a sudden she blinked back salty tears. She put her hands over her eyes to stop them before they rolled down her cheeks. She lifted her chin. "Levi, I can't be anything other than the way I was raised. As much as I love you, I love the Amish church, too. Being with you would mean separation from my family and Old Sam."

Long moments passed while she continued to try for composure. She was usually a good thinker. But right now she wasn't. She threw her hands into the air in frustration. "When I asked God for us to be together, maybe I wanted the impossible."

Sadness loomed between them as Annie tried with desperation to come up with a way to work this out. She'd prayed. But God hadn't answered yet.

"I understand, Annie. But it's the same on this end. We've gone through so much because of what happened. But we could surely compromise, couldn't we? You understand why I can't be Amish."

She considered his words. Finally, the sun hid again behind the clouds. The sad, frustrating mood accompanied the dark gray sky. As Annie looked at him for solace, none came.

They began walking. She fought for a compromise. This was Levi. The boy she'd grown up with. The man she wanted to spend her life with. And he loved her enough to spend the rest of his life with her. There had to be a way for them to be together.

Finally, she stopped and turned to him. There was no way to solve their dilemma. She nearly choked as she took his hand and squeezed it with loving affection. "Good-bye, Levi."

Chapter Ten

That evening, Annie went to her room early. She sat on the edge of her bed and looked down at her dress and apron while she recalled her conversation with Levi and how things had ended.

When a lone tear slipped down her cheek she didn't try to stop it. The image of the devastated expression on Levi's face when she'd told him goodbye was something she'd never forget. And she didn't want to. Memories of their time together were all she had to keep him alive in her mind.

She carefully removed the pin from her hair and lifted her *kapp* just enough to take her precious four-leaf clover between her finger and thumb. With a slow, careful movement, she held it in front of her. Definitely she would save it. But how? The clover would dry and crumble.

An idea came to her, and she put down the small plant on her wooden nightstand and went to her hope chest. She pulled her journal from the beautiful piece and opened it to the last page. Then she sat on her wooden chair and carefully placed the clover between two pages, closing the book on top of it after she made sure the leaves were intact.

She would press it. But she needed something heavier to put on top of the journal to make sure there was enough weight to keep the clover flat while it dried. She looked around the corners of her room, wondering what she had that was heavy enough to make sure the clover pressed. She eyed the flat iron and gave a quick nod of approval. Putting a soft cotton towel between the iron and the cover of the journal, she placed the weight on top. She eyed her project and lifted an uncertain brow. She believed it would work. She knelt at her bedside and folded her arms together.

Squeezing her eyes tightly, she prayed with all her heart. "Dear Lord, forgive me for not having enough faith in You. You know my feelings for Levi, Lord, but You want me to stay in my faith. Please make me whole again. Amen."

The first week of November ended. Levi was sure he and his dad wouldn't start another home till spring. Today they were in the last stages of their final project for the year.

Levi continued his back-and-forth strokes with his brush to the living room ceiling in the four-bedroom home they'd constructed for a newly married man and his wife and her three kids from a former marriage. The image of children running around prompted his lips to curve into a happy grin. He tried to focus on positive thoughts, so he couldn't help imagining this home for himself and Annie and the little ones they would have. With a hopeful breath, he wondered whether their kids would inherit Annie's directness. How many would be boys and the number of girls. Did Annie even want children? He moved his shoulders in a shrug. They'd never discussed it, but he was certain she did.

"Stop," he ordered himself not to go there. To only move forward. He'd often received that advice from his father. Levi knew better than to allow his mind to conjure up things that might never materialize. Because that would only lead to disappointment.

A lone tear stung his eye and he blinked it away. As he considered his last conversation with Annie, his strokes became firmer and swifter. His hand tensed until it cramped.

He set down the brush for a moment and made a fist to rid himself of the uncomfortable sensation. When he continued his work, to his chagrin, the same vision of Annie and their family returned.

As the fresh smell of paint filled the room, he took in the walls. Without thinking, he compared the finished coats with a life with Annie. The unfinished walls were the ones without her.

He swallowed the knot in his throat. As he took in some ugly blotches, he acknowledged that life without Annie would be no different from the unfinished work. Devoid of happiness. And there was nothing he could do to fix it. Emotion ran high as he contemplated her devastating good-bye. His heart had nearly stopped. *What did I expect?*

As he popped open another can of creamy white paint, he pressed his lips together and revisited their last conversation.

He loved her so much. And she loved him. His heart warmed as he could almost hear her sweet, soft voice when she'd so openly confessed her feelings for him.

As a thick drip landed on his forehead, he rubbed it with his shirt sleeve and returned to reality. Sudden emptiness hit him like an ice cold towel to his face. He stopped his work and looked up, not seeing anything except Annie's face.

A dull ache filled his stomach as he tried to reason himself out of his depression. *I'm alone. Without the woman I love with all my heart. But I'm the same Levi Miller I was a month ago, before I went to my cousin's wedding. I was happy then.* He hadn't had any worries, except the unknown reaction to his appearance. He rolled his eyes. How could his life change from happy to sad in such a short time? It didn't make sense. *I've got to get out of this funk. To forget Annie.* Forget he'd spent the past month getting to know her again and admitting he loved her. He shook his head in frustration.

An inquisitive voice interrupted his thoughts. "You're awfully quiet over there." The unexpected words from his dad came from the kitchen. Levi couldn't ignore the clicking of the soles of his father's shoes against the metal bars of the ladder. The wall between the two rooms was partially open, so they could catch glimpses of each other and converse easily.

Levi tried to ignore the comments; the last thing he wanted was to discuss his predicament with the man who was at the crux of the issue. But Levi didn't want to place blame.

To Levi's dismay, his dad pursued the conversation. "You okay?"

"Fine. Just tired," he said, trying to nip the question in the bud.

Silence ensued as Levi dipped his brush into the gallon of paint.

"Well then, son, you've been tired ever since you got home. You can try, but you can't fool your old man. What's eating at you?"

John Miller had been through enough. There was no use reliving it. And the Amish rules couldn't be changed. The *Ordnung* had been the same for years; it wasn't going to suddenly evaporate so Levi could be with Annie.

"I'm glad you're feeling good, son. We've talked about the fire, but we've never discussed what happened during your stay with your aunt and uncle or at the wedding."

"I didn't think you were interested."

Levi saw his father's casual shrug. "Try me. I've been . . . curious. How was everybody?"

"If you mean your brother, he looks the same. Only difference is his beard's gotten pretty long. But you know that. You saw him at the hospital."

Leaning against a piece of drywall, Levi conveyed what he remembered. After he'd recounted a synopsis of the wedding, he threw his hands in the air.

"There's not much else to say." Levi lowered his voice. "All the while, Dad, I was thinking . . ." He hesitated, then dared to speak his mind. "I mean, that it would have been nice if you'd been there."

A sarcastic laugh followed, and an expression that was a combination of amusement and bewilderment crossed the older Miller's sun-darkened face. It always amazed Levi that someone could manage to keep a summer tan all year long. "Put that down." He motioned to Levi's hand. As Levi put the brush into the can of remover to soak, his dad gestured him forward. Levi noted the unusually casual tone of his voice.

An unexpected hand of encouragement on Levi's shoulder startled him. "It's time we sat down and had a man-to-man. It's been a while."

With some hesitation, slow steps took the two of them to the work truck, where the senior Miller stuck his key into the ignition. Levi didn't protest, though he didn't feel ready to discuss his feelings or his no-win situation with Annie. Especially with the man beside him.

"Where are we going, Dad?" Levi checked his watch. "The paint's not done. We can't leave till we . . ."

His father waggled a free hand and made a turnout on the concrete drive and onto the blacktop road leading into town. "Work can wait. This can't. Watching you mope around this past week has been killing me."

"I haven't been moping," Levi said, though he could hear the combination of protest and embarrassment in his voice.

His dad harrumphed. "Then what d'you call it? You've barely eaten. Hardly said two words since you got back home. Your mother's worried you've caught some bug. But you don't look sick; I'd say it's high time we got to the bottom of what's bothering you, and trust me . . ." He breathed in a deep sigh as he pushed the cruise control. "Ain't nothing more important to me than your happiness."

Levi tried to digest that last sentence. His brow rose in surprise, but he didn't reply. The words warmed his heart. John Miller wasn't the type to express emotion. For as long as he could remember, Levi had thought his dad hadn't paid much attention to him. But now he had his father's ear. How much should he say? He tried to decide as gravel crunched under the truck's tires.

While country music oozed from the stereo speakers, Levi's dad slapped a fatherly hand on his shoulder and pressed hard, as if to convey a silent you-know- it-will-be okay message.

"We're headed to the café."

Levi waited for him to continue.

"I'm telling you, son; we're gonna sit down over strong black coffee and get to the root of whatever's nagging at you. And we're not leaving till we fixed you up."

Inside the small, casual joint, his father studied Levi across the booth. "Let's start with the day you came home."

Levi threw up a defensive pair of hands.

"Okay. I'll remind you." He leaned forward. "You

walked into the house after having been gone a month and went straight to your room."

Levi rolled his eyes.

"You can't blow me off, son." John crossed his arms over his chest. "Let's have it."

Annie dried each plate with a vengeance, not leaving a trace of water. After the sink was clean, she'd mop the floor. She'd discovered that staying busy was the only way to keep her mind off Levi. She had to stop dwelling on a future with him. No happily-ever-after this time.

Reality was hard to face right now. She wouldn't even try. She needed to accept that she wouldn't see him again. She yearned to write him, but what would be the point? Being in touch with him would only keep the heartache alive.

She imagined life without him and pulled in a deep, uncertain breath, then pushed it out in desperation when she turned at the gentle touch on her arm.

"Honey, you think you've got a fever?"

Without turning to look Mamma in the eyes, Annie continued the task at hand. "No, Mamma. I'm fine."

"Then what's up with you these days? It's the end of November and you haven't even mentioned Christmas yet."

Finally, Annie dropped what she was doing and faced the woman she loved with all her heart.

"Your appetite has disappeared; why . . ." She

looked Annie up and down and followed with a regretful shake of her head. "Honey, if we don't get you eating again, you're going to . . ." She threw her hands in the air in frustration.

Annie stopped her. "Mamma, don't worry about me. I'm not sick and I'll be okay." She hesitated and added, "In time."

Mamma's brows drew together in a frown. She lowered her voice to avoid being overheard. "This doesn't have anything to do with that Miller boy leaving, now does it? You haven't been yourself ever since . . ."

Annie gave a helpless roll of her eyes. "Mamma, there's no need to look back. He's gone and things are the same as they've always been. In fact, after I clean up the kitchen, I'm gonna pay Old Sam a visit." She forced a smile. "Can't let him go hungry." She stood on her tiptoes to place a dish on the shelf.

But when she reached up, a firm hand stopped her. "This nonsense has to stop, Annie."

She avoided Mamma's gaze. Until her mother placed warm palms on Annie's cheeks and forced her to look at her face. Annie knew she meant business. But that didn't change anything really.

Finally, Annie's voice softened with a combination of regret and sadness. "You told me once, Mamma, that there's no use crying over spilled milk. So I won't. I've got no complaints either. I've been asking God to help me . . ."

Her mom raised a curious brow. "Been asking Him to what?"

Annie waved a dismissive hand. "Oh, nothing."

When Mamma laid a stiff hand on Annie's elbow, Annie sighed regretfully. "I'm just dealing with something. And I appreciate your concern." She put her arms around her role model and offered an affectionate hug. "Really, I do."

"Your daddy and I . . ." Mamma paused to catch a desperate breath. "We want you to be happy."

Annie wasn't sure she could make promises. So, instead, she offered a hopeful shrug and redirected her attention to the countertop.

But to her chagrin, her mother persisted. "You really think a lot of the Miller boy; anyone can see that."

"Doesn't matter. He's not Amish." Annie clenched her fists in frustration. "Levi's wonderful."

Mamma nodded. "Seems like a nice young man." She swallowed. "Can't you appreciate that you caught up with him? Aren't you happy he came back for the wedding?"

Annie thought for a moment. Would she rather not have reconnected with Levi? If he'd stayed away, she wouldn't be going through this torment. Yearning for what she couldn't have.

"I don't know." She changed her mind and snapped her fingers. "Yes, I do. I wish he'd never come home. Because now . . ." She stopped before she said anything else. There was no reason to worry Mamma. Her mother couldn't change the rules.

"You think a lot of him."

Annie gave a slow nod.

"Want some advice?"

Annie offered a slow nod.

"Give it time, Annie. You're of courting age." She lowered her voice so it was barely audible. "I've been noticing how David Stutzman pays you attention. He asked your daddy to court you."

Annie didn't respond.

"Promise me one thing, Annie."

Obediently, Annie waited for her mother to continue.

"That you'll give him a chance."

A couple of days later, Annie returned her flat iron to its original place and anxiously opened her journal to the last page, where she'd placed the clover Levi had given her.

She sat down on the rug next to her bed and smiled in satisfaction. The clover had dried flat. Each leaf was meticulously in place, the way God had made it.

Next, she tried to determine where to keep it. For sure it would have a permanent home in her hope chest, but it would have to be in an envelope so the fragile leaves wouldn't crumble.

With one careful motion, she placed the small plant on a tissue on her bedstand. She would think about how to protect it while she wrote in her journal.

But as she eyed the last page where the clover had been pressed, she raised an astonished brow and pulled the book closer to better examine it. A happy smile tugged at the corners of her lips.

The special clover had left a light imprint. When she eyed the page more carefully, the imprint looked as if it had been professionally placed there. It was like the ghost of the four-leaf clover.

Immediately, she came to a decision. She decided to write about her last visit with Levi. On this page. That way, she could help to preserve what they had said and done, how they'd felt, and keep that day alive. It was the only way she knew how to do it, and the prospect filled her heart with joy. It would be her most precious entry.

She got comfortable, resting her back against the soft quilt Mamma had made, stretched her legs, and wrote. After neatly jotting the date in the upper right-hand corner, she positioned her pen on the top line, pulled in a deep breath, and allowed herself to drift back to that very precious day.

The words flowed over the page. When she reached the end, a lone tear slid down her cheek and landed on the place that detailed her innermost thoughts about Levi Miller. The spot would dry, she figured. But it didn't matter if it didn't. It added emotion to her heartfelt words.

After she finished, a sense of closure filled her chest until she closed her eyes in relief. She'd had her say. Although there was no one she would tell about her feelings for Levi, she had poured out her heart and soul. And writing about her emotions had been a help.

Should she keep this page inside the journal or put it elsewhere?

Levi pulled his feet under the booth. He decided where to start, then met his father's gaze and poured out everything he could think of. When he'd finished, he smiled a little. His problem was far from solved, but he had just unloaded what seemed like a ton of weight he'd been carrying around. His father's expression was thoughtful. Levi was silent, waiting for him to respond.

Finally, his dad gave a slight nod. "I see why you like her, son. She's turned into a beautiful woman. If she's anything like she used to be, she's one determined gal. Never will forget the time she walked to our house to give you herbal tea when you had a cold." An amused grin tugged at the corners of his lips. "In fact, there was something that made her stand out around those shy Amish girls. Perseverance, I'd say. And she spoke her mind." He winked. "She's got that certain sparkle in her eyes." He chuckled. "That one always seemed to be on a mission."

The comment prompted Levi to laugh. "That's an accurate observation. *Always on a mission.* Now that mission is to keep Old Sam fed. She's afraid he'll go hungry. But I'm not worried about him. He's got three girls taking care of him: Annie, Rebecca, and Rachel."

"Then he definitely won't starve."

His dad hesitated and strummed his long fingers against the table. He eyed the half-full coffee cup as if having made some grand decision. Finally, he lowered his voice to a more serious tone. "Son, I understand where you're coming from." The elder Miller lifted his hands, then dropped them on the table. "She's got spunk. And I won't lie to you: Life's never gonna be boring with a gal like that."

He lifted an interested brow and continued. "I

can't tell you how many times they helped me when I needed it."

"Her family?"

A nod followed.

"You were good to them, too."

"Guess you could say they were pretty good friends. Never had complaints against them . . ." He cleared his throat. "Until I was shunned." He gave a strong shake of his head. "I waved to them after I got word from the bishop that I'd broken the rules."

"But, Dad, you knew you were breaking them, right?" Levi couldn't control the pent-up anguish in his voice.

His dad gazed straight ahead. "They didn't wave back."

Levi's jaw dropped. "They didn't?"

A strong shake of the head followed.

"That doesn't sound like them. Maybe they didn't see you? Or do you think they were afraid of being shunned themselves?"

"Don't know. But in Arthur, it's not uncommon for the Amish folks to continue speaking to the shunned."

Levi firmed the tone of his voice. "Dad, I don't agree with shunning. Neither does Annie. But her family might have been afraid to keep on friendly terms with you." Levi shrugged helplessly. "I suppose they worried that they ran the risk of the same thing happening to them. We know from experience that there's no room for negotiating when it comes to the rules."

Then Levi swallowed. "Dad, I've been honest with you. Now come clean with me."

They locked serious gazes.

"I know a little bit about the shunning. But we've never really discussed it in detail." Levi offered an uncertain shrug. Was he out of line, inquiring about something that had devastated his entire family? He was about to find out.

"Son, I've tried all these years to put it behind me. But it seems that's not possible. I never meant to bring us shame."

Levi didn't say anything.

"I guess I got carried away with my business. I'm the one who broke the rules. And I knew better. They've never been a secret."

"You mean you weren't surprised you were shunned?"

Levi watched the tormented expression in his dad's eyes as they sat in silence. For long moments, John's gaze drifted across the café. Levi knew he had asked something that stirred deep emotion. But wasn't it time for answers?

Levi's dad cleared his throat. "Son, it's been over a decade." He gave a firm shake of his head. "I guess it's high time I talk about it."

Several minutes passed before he went on. An uneasy sensation swept through Levi's midsection. He stiffened. But no matter what words came out of his dad now, Levi wanted to hear them. He had to.

"Here's the gist of it. The truck was in my company's name. And of course I'd hired a driver for years. That was all fine and good, but when he quit without notice, I couldn't just cancel all the work my clients were counting on."

Levi moved his palms from the tabletop to his lap.

His fingers shook. "I agree, Dad. But couldn't you make them understand?"

John shrugged. "My situation wasn't quite that simple, son. When my driver quit, yes, I drove while I tried to find a new driver. But the more I drove myself, the more I enjoyed my independence. And the convenience of not having to depend on someone else. It was so easy. Not to mention I saved a lot of money. That was one less person on the payroll."

Levi's jaw dropped. He sat unusually still as he waited for his dad to continue.

"Shunning isn't something that happens fast. Or without repeated warnings. I was warned and given chances to repent."

"Dad . . ."

John threw up his hands. "I admit I was selfish. And today, I wish I'd handled the situation differently. What I did hurt our entire family."

Levi's heart jumped with surprise. He couldn't believe what he was hearing.

"Son, I supported a family. But that wasn't the only reason I did what I did." He softened the tone of his voice to a note of regret. "I suppose my ambition was too big for Arthur, Illinois. And today I can sit here and tell you that I have no regrets."

Levi pressed his cold palms against his thighs and leaned forward. Then he paused to gather his composure. His pulse pumped to a hard, heavy beat of disbelief as he tried to keep his voice down so as not to draw attention to himself.

The man sitting opposite him had explained what had happened and where he stood as if it were merely another fact of life. Levi studied his face. His father's cheeks didn't show any extra color. He sat there calmly, as if he'd just explained that he was thirsty. For long moments, Levi tried to respond, but no words would leave his mouth.

As if sensing Levi's disbelief, his dad went on. "Son, they did what they believed was right. And shunning . . . I know it's harsh and I wouldn't do it, but it's not meant to harm the person. It's meant to be redemptive. And many times the person they avoid will repent and be accepted back into the community. I chose not to."

Levi knew his dad didn't understand that he wasn't shocked that the Amish had shunned him in the first place but was way overcome with dismay that all the while he had known it was coming. And despite what they would eventually go through, which had been complete devastation, he'd stuck to his plan anyway.

Finally, Levi gave a frustrated roll of his eyes and leaned forward. "So it was really your choice not to stay Amish. Do I understand that correctly?"

A thoughtful nod followed an uncertain shrug. "When you put it that way, it sounds so logical." Finally, his words were barely audible. "Yes, son. I knew it would happen."

"You never believed that going outside the *Ordnung* was wrong?"

After a few moments, John took a swig of coffee and smiled. "At first I wasn't sure. But the more I drove my truck, the more I read the Bible, son. The way you interpret it is the key. The Amish translate it literally. In fact, years before they gave me the boot, I questioned some of the practices. For instance, it doesn't make sense to me that they'll ride in cars but not own or drive them."

Levi sat unusually still and continued to listen.

"In this world, it's difficult to interpret the Bible word for word. Because when you do that, there are contradictions. Use your logic, son. Everything isn't black and white, and I'm sure God doesn't expect perfection from us."

These calm statements from his father about such a serious subject made Levi's heart beat to a reckless, anxious speed. He thought of all that the shunning had forced on him. Of what it had done to him and Annie. Of the barrier it still made between them. Yet, his dad seemed emotionless as he discussed it.

"When it happened, I was just a man doing my best to follow God and support a family at the same time. I agreed with some of the rules, but not all of them."

To Levi's surprise, his father leaned forward and grabbed Levi by his forearms. In an especially tender voice, he said, "Levi, you're a grown man. I know things might seem complicated now, but you'll see one day, when you raise your own family, it's impossible to do everything according to the Bible. The honest truth is, you have to do your best for yourself and your family."

"But, Dad . . ."

The grasp on Levi's arms became stronger. More intense. And so was the emotion that sparked in his father's eyes. "Son, I don't have the answers to all of life's questions. But our Heavenly Father does. And what you feel about Annie?" After a brief hesitation, he gave a reassuring nod. "I think that what you feel for the girl will blow over in time. There are lots of pretty young gals around. Say your prayers at night like we always taught you. Ask our Lord what to do. Right now, you may not know. But in time, you'll figure it out. And you've got my support, whatever you decide."

Chapter Eleven

David Stutzman hitched up his horse and helped Annie into the black buggy. She'd never had so much fun at the singings. While she moved across the seat, she contemplated her conversation with Mamma about giving it a go with David. Maybe Mamma was right.

To Annie's astonishment, tonight had been the first time she'd been able to put Levi out of her mind. An assortment of stars and an unusually bright moon decorated the early November sky. The coolness of the evening prompted her to wrap her arms around herself. Between her coat and the softness of the quilt on David's bench seat, she began to get warm.

Beside her, David laughed. "Sometimes I think them English got somethin' right."

Annie darted him a questioning glance.

"Tonight would be mighty fine to be driving a car and feel that heat oozing out of the vents, don't ya think?"

Annie smiled at the thought. She knew what that

warmth felt like. She'd experienced it the times she'd gotten rides to the hospital when her cousin's baby was born. Besides, some Amish had gas heaters inside their buggies. Her daddy did. She wished David did, too.

"Ya ever think about having a car, Annie?"

The innocent question prompted Annie to smile. "I wouldn't want one, no. I prefer horse and buggy, hands down. For one thing, I don't want an insurance bill. I've heard they're pretty steep. But even if I had the money to pay the bill, this is what I know and love." She giggled and added, "However . . . tonight some heat would be nice."

He agreed.

The buggy creaked and bumped as they took the blacktop home. Eventually, David worked his way into the queue. There were several buggies behind them.

"I've been hearin' 'bout those sponge cakes you make for Old Sam." He grinned. "It's no secret 'round here that Sam claims your sponge cakes would give his Esther's a run for her money."

The admission took Annie's breath away. She beamed, resting a modest hand over her heart, which had nearly jumped right out of her chest. "Really?"

"Uh-huh."

"That's a pretty strong compliment."

"To tell the truth, I really don't know much about you." He paused. "'Cept you make those good desserts."

The buggy jumped a little as they turned to get on

the main road into town. Annie adjusted in her seat for a more comfortable position.

"What other hobbies you got, Ms. Annie?"

Enjoying the peaceful ride, she clasped her hands together thoughtfully. When she released them, she placed her palms on her thighs. "I like growing my own herbs." Annie didn't want to talk about herself too much. It was time to ask David a bit about himself. She wasn't terribly interested, but it was common courtesy. Besides, he was certainly pleasant. And he liked her enough to court her.

She threw the question back to him. "How about you, David? What do you enjoy?"

He chuckled. "Everything on my dad's farm. The Lord's been good to me that way. Got no complaints."

"Livestock must take up most of your time. Dad tells me you and your papa have over a hundred hogs now."

"*Jah.*" He glanced at her, his eyes wide with pride. "Sure you heard that we supply most of the town with ham on the holidays."

He lifted his chin. As she eyed him, she took in his humble expression and realized how much she'd thought of him. She was sure he'd make a loyal and hardworking husband to some lucky girl.

Annie sighed and relaxed her shoulders. As she crossed her legs at the ankles, she and David continued to chitchat as the carriage traversed the winding blacktop. She'd noted the distinct smell of cinnamon and wondered where it came from.

Her answer came when she noticed a couple of hot red plastic coverings near David's feet. She smiled a little. She was sure they were wrappings from the sundries shop. Sometimes, after selling fresh veggies in the summer, she'd taken her horse and buggy into town to buy candy treats for her daddy.

Annie considered David and decided she enjoyed his open-book personality. She admitted that it would be difficult to be sad around someone so jovial and doubted he ever complained about anything.

A comfortable silence ensued while they wound around the part of the road that faced the mouth of Pebble Creek. Without warning, a dull ache swept into Annie's chest, filling it until she thought it would burst with pain.

She fought the agony; certainly she couldn't ruin their nice evening. He was such a kind person, and he hadn't done anything to deserve her spoiling the night.

As Pebble Creek loomed in the distance, memories of Levi flooded Annie's mind until her head pounded as if a gas-powered jackhammer was piercing rocky ground. She recalled the wonderful times they'd met at their secret spot. But tonight she wouldn't be seeing the man who had left town for good. The guy she loved with everything she had was no longer a member of her family's church.

"You've gotten awfully quiet."

Ashamed, she sat up straighter and forced a smile. "I'm sorry. I was just taking in the evening. It was wonderful."

David's reaction was that of relief. A brief silence

passed before he lowered his voice to a low, breathy tone. "Annie, uh, I really like you a lot."

The evening had just gone south. And it wasn't David's fault. Now her chest ached with guilt. With regret that nothing could ever be different between them. She had tried. She had set her mind to do what was impossible. She owed him an explanation. But how could she tell him without hurting his feelings? It had been a mistake to even think about courting him. She prepared her words. "David, I like you, too."

Even in the dark, when he glanced her way she could see sparkles in his eyes. Rosy cheeks that became rounder when he smiled.

"You're a good friend," she added.

This time, his laugh was edged with nervousness.

"Of course I'm your friend, Annie." He cleared his throat before continuing. "But I really think a lot of you; I want us to spend time together, if that's okay."

Honesty was her only choice. She hated saying what needed to be said. She gathered her strength and spoke in her most gentle, sympathetic tone. "David, I've enjoyed this evening more than you'll ever know. But all we can be is friends." She hesitated and continued on a more upbeat note. "I want that very much."

He let out a sigh and gave a slight nod. "It's that Miller guy, isn't it?" Before Annie could speak, David continued his train of thought. "I heard you two was gettin' close at the wedding."

Annie's heart pumped harder and harder. So her feelings for Levi were no secret in the community.

But she wouldn't confirm them. That sentiment was something she wouldn't share with others. What was the point when nothing could come of it? Besides, if she discussed her feelings for Levi with David, it would get back to Mamma, and the last thing she wanted to do was upset her.

"David, any girl would be honored to spend time with you. I know there's some lucky gal just waiting to court you."

His laugh was relaxed and accepting. "I've always heard you're direct, Annie. And I sure like that about you. Ya know what? I still want to be friends with you."

Her heart warmed. She turned to him. "*Jah?*"

He nodded. "You're fun to be with. And I appreciate your honesty." He waved an understanding hand. "Really, I do. I'd like to do things with you every once in a while, but in the meantime, I'll keep my eyes open for the real deal. And you do the same. How's that?"

The next evening, Annie thought back on her outing with David. Mamma seemed happy enough that they'd gone to the singing.

On the surface, Annie guessed things looked all right. And that made her happy. The last thing she wanted was to worry her parents. Why couldn't she just fall in love with a good Amish boy the way Mamma had fallen in love with Daddy?

Annie gave a dismissive shrug and cut the wick on her kerosene lantern. As soon as she lit the flame, she carefully placed it on her bedroom floor. She was always careful to keep the light away from anything that could start a fire. The room certainly wasn't bright, but there was definitely enough light for reading and for writing in her journal. She removed her *kapp* and hairpins, allowing loose strands of hair to caress her tense shoulders.

As she went through the evening ritual of hanging her black dress on the hook and replacing it with a pale blue nightgown, she thought of everything going on in her life. Slow, thoughtful steps took her to her hope chest, where she stopped to take in a deep, appreciative breath.

Despite all the uncertainty and challenges, one thing was constant. That was Old Sam. She gazed with wonder at the recipe he had so artfully etched into the beautifully stained wood. As light from the lantern flickered, she traced her finger over the engraved letters and smiled as she finally opened the lid.

Inside, she reached for her journal and pen. When she touched the lined pages, it was as if she held a part of herself.

Leaving the lid open to admire the natural grains in the oak, she clutched the book to her chest and squeezed her eyes closed.

She still wasn't sure what to do about her feelings for Levi, but tonight, while she wrote, she expected to come to a very important decision. So much was at stake.

For long moments she studied the blank page in

front of her and wondered how to begin. Finally, she put pen to paper.

During the past weeks, I've been fighting a terrible ache in my heart. Tonight, I'm on the verge of deciding the next step in my life. Although I want with all my heart to join the Amish church and raise my children the way I was raised, I can't settle for a husband I don't truly love.

I've been told many times that the Amish place great importance on choosing a spouse who works hard. That anyone can buy material things and give them, but that labor and helping with children speak of true love.

It seems to me that our faith places more emphasis on what's practical than emotions. But . . .

She paused.

When I'm with Levi, my heart . . . flutters. Levi is a hard worker, too. When I'm with him, I smile. I laugh. I feel something so wonderful, it can only be true love. I have always been raised to believe that with God, anything is possible. That's why I know He'll make a way for me to be with Levi.

She paused to look up and tapped the end of her pen nervously against her leg.

Should I sacrifice the only true love I've ever known for my church? Surely my Heavenly Father wouldn't want me to throw away something so precious just because Levi's father broke the rules. God is forgiving. I don't understand why the very people I have grown to love and respect over the years were so hard on John Miller for something that didn't hurt anyone.

Frustrated, she stood and made her way to the window, where she took in the bright little stars. In the distance, scattered throughout the sky, were miracles of God, but she knew their placement wasn't a coincidence. God had carefully determined where each would rest. It must be the same with His people, she reasoned. He must have put Levi in her life again for a reason.

When she returned to her seat, she wrote with more decisiveness.

Levi is a believer, just like me. He worships the same God. Surely he isn't at fault for what his father did. In my heart, I believe God will work this out for us. God responds to prayers and He'll answer mine.

As a moonbeam slipped in through the window to compete with the dim light from the lantern, a new sense of calm swept through Annie. She rested her head against the mattress and thought of her time with Levi at Pebble Creek. She imagined being in Katie's place at the wedding, with Levi at her side. She smiled and knew what to write.

I want to marry Levi. To attend church with him. Raise children together. To cook him special dinners. Clean house for him. I want a family more than anything in the world. But tonight, as I gaze at the stars,

I've decided to stay true to what I've been taught. God's plan for me is much larger than my plan for myself. I have to trust Him. I have heard so many times to have faith. Now I'm being tested. In staying true to what I believe, I may have to sacrifice my own happiness. If I can't marry the man I truly love, I won't marry at all. God surely won't punish me for that. I realize true love is a blessing. Not everyone who finds it is able to keep it. But I've experienced that blessed feeling I always dreamed of since I was a child.

She turned another page and returned her pen to the blank paper.

I won't do what my parents don't wish me to do. I certainly believe God doesn't want me to marry a man simply because he is of the same church. And He surely doesn't desire for me to marry anyone other than my true love.

She knew her world wouldn't be perfect without Levi. But she would make the most of her life. As far as children, she would love her nieces and nephews as if they were her own. She would hold their babies. Teach them to read and write.

And Levi will always be in my heart. And I'll pray that he'll find true love with someone else.

As she closed the journal, fresh tears slid down her cheeks. She didn't wipe them away. They were a combination of sadness and relief. She'd just resolved to give up what she loved most for God.

Her heart ached. A huge void loomed within her as she sadly contemplated the rest of her life. Would she find happiness that even half matched the joy between her and Levi? Surely God wouldn't let her entire future be miserable simply because of a sacrifice she'd made for the church that meant everything to her.

She couldn't be with Levi. At the same time, she didn't have to keep all this inside her. There had to be someone she could share her situation with besides Old Sam. Surely there was someone she could talk to. Someone who wouldn't judge her or think less of her. A listener who would understand and empathize and possibly even offer advice. She immediately thought of Mamma, then gave a strong shake of her head. Her sister? Sighing, Annie gave a frustrated roll of her eyes.

To her surprise, Old Sam had merely encouraged her to figure things out with her own heart. Her heart warmed with respect. She could share this with him; however, he wouldn't be able to empathize with her. As wise and astute as he was, she doubted he could respond in a way that would help her cope with the situation. Her dilemma was something only a woman would understand.

But she didn't want to risk being gossiped about in her tight-knit community. She pressed her palms against the hardwood floor on either side of her.

I can't put my family's hard-earned respect in jeopardy. The very knowledge that I've fallen in love with someone outside the faith would follow them forever. Especially if it involved the only son of John Miller.

Shunning happened rarely, which was the reason it was so talked about. And gossip was evil. She thought highly of her church friends, but unfortunately, they had very long memories. But no doubt about it, she needed a sounding board.

Annie eyed the stars that decorated the dark sky. There must be someone she could talk to who could lead her in the right direction. If nothing else, she sought a way to look at the end of her relationship with Levi, accept the inevitable, and move on.

But who?

Annie's jaw dropped in amazement as she stepped inside Rebecca Conrad's arched front door. Annie was sure her eyes must be as large as the state of Texas as she viewed the wide circular stairwell leading to the second story and the beautifully designed ceilings that sported a different shade from the cinnamon-colored walls. Dark oak woodwork contrasted with off-white ceilings in a stunning way.

The Conrads' new home seemed like a mansion compared to Annie's modest dwelling. With a welcoming smile, newly married Rebecca motioned her inside.

Annie handed Rebecca the plate of sponge cakes she'd baked for her and William. "They look delicious!" She winked at Annie before adding in a mock serious tone, "And rumor has it they taste every bit as good as they look!"

While Annie watched Rebecca carefully set the

creamy white porcelain dish on a nearby table, Annie considered her comment.

"By rumor, I assume you mean Old Sam?"

They both laughed. Rebecca came to Annie and widened her arms in an affectionate embrace. When they hugged, Annie inhaled the potent rose scent on Rebecca's dark blue sleeves. Inside, Annie smiled. Even Rebecca's clothes smelled of flowers.

It was no secret Old Sam loved Annie's sponge cakes as much as Rebecca's wildflower bouquets.

"Of course. By the way he talks, I'm sure he could live on them. In fact . . ." She pressed a finger to her lips and lowered her eyes so her pupils were partially hidden. "It's my guess he watches out of his barn window all day, waiting for you to come."

That made Annie laugh. "I try to take good care of him. I love him so much." She drew her arms over her chest and threw back her head.

"I know you do. So do I . . . although I'm sure my bouquets can't compete with your edibles. I spent a little time with him yesterday." Hands on hips, she raised her chin a notch. "Oh, Annie, I just love what he does with those hope chest lids. He's a true artist."

"No one would argue with that."

"It's so good to see you," she exclaimed, holding her at arm's length. "How have you been?"

The newlywed's smile seemed to light up her entire unblemished face. In her *kapp* and dark blue dress, she looked like perfection. And according to everything Annie knew about her, she was.

"I'm so glad for the opportunity to see your new

home. It's . . ." Annie threw her hands up in a speechless gesture. "Gorgeous!"

Growing up, Rebecca had always seemed to succeed with everything she did. It was common knowledge her tomatoes were the best in the area. Her red bell peppers, too. And she was an acclaimed giver of advice; somehow, logic had been built into her character, as if it belonged there. And to top things off, her pot roast couldn't be matched by even the elders in the community. So really, why should Annie be surprised that this lovely girl lived in this extraordinary home?

"Please have a seat." Rebecca's brows drew together in a frown as she motioned to the cluttered table. "There's a lot going on here right now. Hope you don't mind the mess."

Automatically, Annie glanced at the colorful dried flowers and stems arranged in neat little piles. To her amazement, the mélange of hues looked as if they went with the dark-stained oak table. From Annie's peripheral vision, she noted small pots of young green plants on the windowsills. Deep green vines dangled over the sides of the terra-cotta pots hanging from the ceiling. If Annie hadn't known better, she'd think she was in a plant store. She had to remind herself this was a residence. The pleasant-smelling aroma added to the homey appearance.

Annie closed her eyes in delight as she breathed in the mellow, sweet floral scent that floated in the air. An automatic smile lifted the corners of her lips in reaction to the pleasant smells. Rebecca's dining room made Annie think of Allerton Park, the well-known tourist site she had once visited with a group of friends. The attraction boasted an array of beautiful gardens.

Remembering her reason for coming, Annie said, "I heard your business is doing well."

Rebecca nodded with a raised brow. "To be honest, it's a nice surprise. But it's taking off so fast, I hope I can keep up!"

She sighed with delight. "Oh, Annie, I absolutely love making wreaths, from raising the flowers to drying them to choosing the best materials and arranging them to look good. I enjoy the fragrances and making each one with a different theme. It's amazing the beauty God created, and it costs nothing!"

Annie nodded in agreement. "They say the best things in life are free."

"God gives us so many blessings, Annie. And money can't buy them."

"I think sometimes people are too wrapped up in material things. And all they have to do is step outside and look at what God gave us."

"I'm so grateful for everything I have, Annie. And now?" She raised her palms to the ceiling. "I'm living my dream of creating floral arrangements. To be honest, I've wanted it for a long time. But in my heart of hearts, I didn't believe it would materialize. But you know . . . I never dreamed there would be such a demand for dried arrangements."

"Really? I mean, you didn't think you'd start a business?"

Rebecca shook her head. "Not here. We Amish aren't too hip on flowers, but customers hear about my products through word of mouth." She rested her hands on her hips. "And I'm loving it!"

As if remembering something, Rebecca paused. "My! I almost forgot to put my pot roast in the oven." She stepped quickly to the kitchen. Her voice echoed back to Annie from the nearby room. "Give me a moment and I promise to be right back," she hollered from the other side of the wall. "I get so wrapped up in my flowers, sometimes I forget everything else."

"No hurry!"

Annie smiled and studied the table with curious eyes. Rebecca's dream was coming true. For a few blissful moments, Annie's mind wandered to a place that would allow her to pursue and get her own.

She bent forward to touch the light pink rose petal. To Annie's surprise, it was still soft. The floral colors before her were gorgeous hues that reminded her of a painter's canvas. What amazed her was that dead plants could look so lovely.

As Annie regarded the petals, she struggled to imagine a world where she could accomplish her own goal. But what was it? The question challenged her. Unlike Rebecca, she didn't have something in mind as daring as starting a business. All she wanted, really, was to marry, have a family, and raise her children with the man she loved. It was what many yearned for. But even so, that particular goal wasn't simple. Not for her anyway. Automatically, she thought of Levi and her heart jumped. She imagined her and Levi in front of several hundred guests.

But flowers wouldn't play a role in her wedding. Such decorations weren't part of Amish festivities. And why would she even dare to envision Levi dressed up next to her?

She squeezed her eyes closed and ordered herself to stop imagining what could never be. Her shoulders tensed. She breathed a deep sigh of defeat. Why on earth had she allowed herself to go there? With a frustrated roll of her eyes, she forced the forbidden longing from her mind and focused on her friend's success.

Rebecca's return brought Annie back to reality. She eyed her friend's small bump. "When's the baby due?"

Rebecca sat. "February. I never imagined how wonderful carrying a little one could make me feel." She drew her arms over her body and let out a happy sigh. "I don't know what I ever did to deserve such happiness, Annie." Her voice was edged with breathlessness. "William is over the moon. The two of us . . . In fact, both of us are unusually emotional. I tell you . . ."

Then she threw her hands in the air in an unexplainable gesture. "Being pregnant is more exciting than I ever dreamed it would be. I'm with the man I've loved forever. Soon we'll have a little one." She glanced at the living room. "We've built this beautiful home. My family's right next door."

She paused before raising her voice with excitement. "I go to bed at night thanking God for all He's given me." Her eyes suddenly sparkled with moisture. "What more could a girl ask for?"

Annie shrugged. "Nothing. You're blessed."

"You will be too, Annie. Somehow, I just know it. And when that time comes, you'll know what I'm talking about. Why look at you!" Rebecca spread her arms. "You've got the world at your doorstep."

Annie swallowed the lump in her throat. It wasn't because she wasn't happy for this special woman. She was. But she wasn't sure she would ever be in Rebecca's position. Even her voice sparkled. Happiness emanated from the woman who had left their community during *Rumspringa* to help the man who was now her husband run his ailing father's cabinetry business. She had even left the state of Illinois! *Jah*, she was the perfect person to talk to about her forbidden love.

"It's hard to believe that only a short time ago, I thought none of this would happen."

Seated opposite her, Rebecca organized the dried flowers and leaves littering the table so there was more room. After Rebecca shoved some piles out of the way, she eyed Annie. "What would you like to drink? I made a fresh pot of tea. How about a glass?"

"I'll have one with you."

Rebecca slipped into the kitchen and returned with two glasses filled with ice and beverage. She placed one on a coaster in front of Annie and the other on her own place mat.

"I hope you don't mind, but there's something I came to talk to you about," Annie began. "It's . . . confidential."

Rebecca winked. "I'm a good secret keeper." Suddenly, her lips dropped and the tone of her voice changed. "I hope your family's all right. Your mamma . . ."

Annie gave an immediate shake of her head. "My folks are fine. And really, it's nothing having to do with health. It's personal." She cleared her throat, feeling embarrassed. She felt a bit selfish coming to busy Rebecca for a problem about herself but desperately needed to confide her dilemma or she would go crazy. She carefully considered her next words, then she straightened her shoulders and lifted her chin, looking straight into her friend's intense eyes. "Rebecca, you've got it all." She glanced from side to side. "And your relationship with William; well, it seems too good to be true. But was there ever a time when you had something come between you?"

When Rebecca didn't respond, Annie went on. "I'm sure your relationship must have been challenged in some way when you helped William's dad in Indiana."

Rebecca hesitated. "*Challenged* is putting it mildly," she finally said. "Annie, I came close to losing him. Everything."

Annie sat up straight with interest. Despite the serious confession, she smiled with relief. "I knew I could talk to you, Rebecca. You're the one person who might understand what I'm going through with Levi Miller."

Rebecca lifted a surprised brow.

"When we were kids, Levi and I were best friends."

Rebecca's eyes lit up as she took a drink and returned her glass to the wooden coaster, ice cubes jiggling. "I remember. You guys were practically joined at the hip."

Annie lowered her gaze to the table and fidgeted with her hands on her lap. She tapped the toe of her black shoe against the shiny hardwood floor. Moments later, she met Rebecca's gaze and went on. "As you know, he was back for the wedding."

Rebecca nodded eagerly. "We were so happy to see him."

"Me too. It gave us a chance to catch up."

Rebecca stopped what she was doing and sat very still. Annie took in the uncertain expression on her face, as if she wasn't sure what to expect.

Annie's voice cracked with emotion. "And, Rebecca, something happened. Something so wrong."

Rebecca's jaw dropped.

Annie's chest pumped up and down as if she'd been running too fast. Catching her breath, she cleared her throat. Trying to focus on the most important parts, Annie told the woman across the table what had happened. She spoke in such rushed phrases, she wondered if Rebecca could understand everything. Finally, Annie was finished. A sigh of relief escaped her as her back met the hard chair. She had voiced her troubles; it felt good to get them off her chest.

"Please don't think badly of me, Rebecca, but . . ." Salty moisture stung her eyes and she blinked. "I'm in love with Levi. I can't help it."

A long, tense silence ensued. While Rebecca pressed her lips together, Annie's heart continued to pump to a wild, uncertain beat. She'd just confessed the unthinkable. Suddenly, she wasn't certain she'd made the right decision in coming here with her problem. Had she made a mistake? Surely Rebecca wouldn't tell anyone what she'd admitted?

As the delicious-smelling aroma of cooked pork began to fill the room, Rebecca looked away; her brows narrowed. For something to do, Annie swallowed another sip of tea, but the liquid barely made it down her throat. Unable to finish, she returned the glass to the table and clasped her hands in her lap, awaiting a response.

Finally, Rebecca gave a sympathetic shake of her head. "Annie, I would *never* think badly of you." She inhaled and went on. "I'm a straight shooter, just like you. In fact, in many ways we're a lot alike. And I like to credit myself for being a problem solver." Her jaw tightened. "You're certainly not in an easy situation; as much as I'd like to, I don't think I can come up with a quick, logical answer."

She gazed at Annie and said, "I have a secret of my own."

Annie sat up even straighter.

"I think it's time for me to tell you what happened to William and me in Indiana."

Annie waited with keen interest as Rebecca moved in her chair, then took a stem between her fingers to play with it while she spoke. "It always helps to commiserate with someone when you're in a pinch. And if my instincts are right, it might help you decide which path is best for something so difficult as wanting to spend your life with someone outside the faith." She paused. "William's dad and stepmom—they're English, you know."

Annie offered a firm nod. She'd heard bits and pieces about the couple over the years.

"Wasn't he shunned for marrying outside of the faith? I know a little bit about it. Didn't it happen soon after his wife passed away?"

"Uh-huh."

Annie's heart picked up speed. "I want to hear

everything about Indiana. And you have my word that what you say will stay in this room."

Rebecca put down the stem and with a slow, careful motion, moved her glass of tea away. She clasped her palms together on the table and drew in a small sigh. "It all started when William's dad suffered a heart attack and couldn't keep up with his business. William's stepmom, Beth, asked if William could help. Of course he agreed. And because I loved William, I wanted to pitch in. Even if I couldn't do anything else, I'd be moral support. I was concerned for William. He'd never been out of this town."

"And you went."

"I did. But you can't believe the hurdles I jumped to go." She gave a slow shake of her head. "Even though I was in *Rumspringa*, getting approval wasn't easy." She looked away. When she returned her focus to Annie, the expression on her eyes had taken on a new, even more serious depth. "I mean, I had never left my folks. William and I weren't married. There were other things to consider, too. My absence meant that someone would have to cover my chores while I was away. And to go and live with an English family?"

Annie grinned at the funny way Rebecca rolled her eyes.

"Because I was in *Rumspringa*, my parents and the bishop *finally* gave me their blessing." She leaned forward in her chair and their gazes locked. "As long as I met certain conditions." She shook her head and waved a hand. "But that's a story for another day."

Annie giggled. Despite the seriousness of the

conversation, the way Rebecca told the story held a certain humor. "What happened? Was it hard living in a different culture?"

Rebecca lifted a brow. "Not for me. In fact, now that it's over, I look back and realize what a great learning experience it was. A blessing. In more ways than one. Because of the dilemma I faced with William, the time with the Conrads made me a much better person. I'm stronger than ever." She lowered her eyes to the tabletop. When she met Annie's gaze again, the look on her face was intense. "We all deal with things differently. But William . . ." Rebecca cleared her throat and downed some tea. "The experience confused him."

Before Annie could ask how, Rebecca went on. "I mean about how we live. It was such a sharp contrast from his folks' way of life."

Annie gave a slow nod of understanding.

"I was surprised and a bit taken aback when William began criticizing our faith. He started second-guessing how we do things. In fact, he forgot why we sacrifice so much to follow our beliefs. To make things simple, the English lifestyle appealed to him. Too much."

"Oh."

"Trust me, I didn't know if we would wind up together because he seriously considered leaving the Plain Faith to live like his dad and stepmom."

"No!"

Rebecca gave a slight nod. "Temptations from every direction pulled at William and I couldn't reason with him. He especially wanted a car. And the TV? It became his best friend. I couldn't tear him away from the sports channel." Rebecca folded her hands in her lap. "He fell in love with Beth's red automobile. She even taught him to drive."

Annie pressed her palms to her cheeks as she stared at the woman across the table. "I had no idea you went through such a struggle. What did you say? What did you do?"

Rebecca harrumphed. "What options were there? I was in a pinch. I wrote to Old Sam and he returned my letter, but at the end of the day, even he didn't have a black-and-white answer." She paused and lowered her voice. "But throughout the ordeal, there was one person I turned to." She pointed a finger up to the ceiling. "I relied on my faith to get me through it, and to be honest, I wasn't sure the ending was going to be what I wanted. I tried to see things through William's perspective. And in many ways, I understood."

"You did?"

Rebecca nodded. "I couldn't begrudge him feeling the way he did. For heaven's sake, we're only human; that means he doesn't have to always see things my way and I don't have to think like him. Besides . . ." She gave a casual lift of her hands, then let them fall into her lap. "We were in *Rumspringa* after all; becoming members of the faith is an important step, and if there was doubt in William's mind about joining the church, that was definitely the time to figure it out. The uncertainty . . ." She gave a firm shake of her head. "It wasn't something I would want to go through again. But despite my anxiety, in my heart I wanted William to be satisfied." She lowered her voice to a more confidential tone. "Though selfishly, I wanted him to be happy with me at his side."

Annie's jaw dropped as she digested Rebecca's surprising words. "I don't blame you."

As if understanding Annie's confusion, Rebecca leaned back in her chair and darted her friend a sympathetic look. "As I explain this, I know it sounds crazy, but if you had been there, Annie, you would have understood." She cleared her throat. "The Conrads are wonderful people. And I love them." A laugh escaped her. "How could I not?" Rebecca clasped her hands together on the table. "Beth was so kind. She went out of her way to make sure I was comfortable. I love that woman to death. And William's dad?" She moved her hands to her lap. "I couldn't help but care for him. His heart condition really took a toll. And whether he would make it or not was questionable. Thank goodness he survived. Beth and Daniel; they're great. But how they live . . ."

Rebecca gave a casual lift of her shoulders. "By no means do I mean to be critical. After all, they're English. Like us, they follow their hearts. But, Annie?"

Annie waited.

"I would be lying if I said they didn't have everything at their fingertips." Rebecca squinted as she eyed the tiny stem between her fingertips. "Privileges we're not used to. For instance, when Beth goes to the store, she simply climbs in her car and turns the ignition. There's no hitching up a horse to a buggy. And when it's warm outside, they flip the switch on the wall that turns on the air. You get the picture."

Annie gave a quick nod.

"These things aren't bad, but their system is so different from what we're used to."

"System. That's an interesting way to put it. But were you really surprised?" Annie moved forward to the edge of her seat. "You knew these material things were around; we go to Walmart and Sears, just like everyone else."

"I know. We see Maytags, large-screen televisions; we're not immune to cars; I mean, we ride in them when necessary. But I guess what I'm getting at is that you get a totally different picture of English life when you actually live in that world." She put her hand over her mouth as a small laugh came out. "I suppose you could compare the differences to a swimming pool."

Annie lifted a curious brow.

"It's different watching from the shore from actually being in the water."

Annie smiled. "I understand. But didn't you like it?"

"The lifestyle?"

Annie nodded.

Rebecca laughed. "Who wouldn't?"

Annie joined in the laughter.

"I've always appreciated battery-run fans in my dad's cabinet shop, but I'm telling you: after working in the Conrad shop all day, air conditioning felt so good at night. You know, there's even a Jacuzzi in the guest bathroom."

Annie's eyes widened.

"Have you ever heard of such a thing?" Before Annie could respond, Rebecca added, "And, Annie, when I sat in it, the water from the jets felt like heaven against my feet. And after I added the bath gel, the entire room smelled of lavender."

Annie took in Rebecca's dreamy expression as she paused.

"There were so many comforts! Looking back, I guess I shouldn't have been surprised at how quickly William took to the oversize flat-screen television. He had the channel clicker in the palm of his hand as often as time allowed. And Beth's double oven?" Rebecca let out a low whistle. "It was a dream come true."

Annie giggled.

Rebecca's lips lifted into a smile. "In fact, it's what I miss the most." Her eyes sparkled with amusement.

When she continued, her voice was serious. "But all the while, Annie, I realized that material things aren't what I'm about. I didn't allow myself to become attached because I viewed them as temptations." She shrugged. "Temporary pleasures. So when I left, giving them up wasn't all that difficult. Besides, love for my faith prevented me from ever considering changing what I have. That said, after seeing William react in his own way, I realized how much discipline it takes to live the way we do. And to be honest . . ." She shrugged. "I'm happy."

Annie nodded. "I guess we're pretty tough when you consider everything we go through to stay in the faith."

Rebecca squeezed her eyes closed a moment, and when she opened them, Annie noticed moisture sparkling there. It reminded her of morning dew on a leaf. She respected and admired this young woman for confessing such a unique experience.

"Annie, struggles aren't easy. They test us. I was fortunate to come out of that situation with William by my side. But through the process, I learned a lot about myself. At first I saw the challenges as a bad thing. Something I didn't want. I couldn't imagine living without William. To me, there was no plan B."

"Of course not."

She leaned forward. "But, Annie, you know what I learned?"

"What?"

"That challenges aren't all bad; we get through them. And there's a reason behind every hardship."

"Why do you think that happened to you?"

"In Indiana, God tested my strength."

Annie considered the statement. She took a deep breath of astonishment. She couldn't believe Rebecca looked back at what had almost robbed her of true love with such levelheadedness. Annie wasn't sure she had the strength to make it through such an ordeal.

"I'm not saying it was easy." She gave a strong shake of her head. "Not at all! Annie, I prayed so many times for William to stay in the faith." She clenched her fists. "Prayed with everything I had. But as the days passed, it was clear William was bent on becoming English."

Annie rolled her eyes in amazement.

"I was more afraid of losing him than I'd ever been of anything in my entire life. And I was at a huge disadvantage."

Annie lifted a curious brow.

"Old Sam wasn't there for me to talk to!"

They laughed.

"As I said, I wrote him, and he responded of course. But to my surprise, there was nothing he could do to spare me the pain or struggle. It surprised me. I thought he had a solution for the worst things imaginable!"

"Oh!"

"Anyway, as the time to come home grew closer, William and I talked about which way we were headed. About our relationship." Rebecca's voice was edged with drama. "He actually asked me to become English."

Annie's jaw dropped in amazement. "No!"

"I told him I couldn't."

Annie thought for a moment. "But you're married now. Obviously the two of you worked things out. Something must have happened and I can't wait to find out what it was!"

Rebecca looked away before she offered a quick nod. "But I nearly lost William in the process. It seemed as if everything worked against my marriage to him. In fact, during all the chaos, Daniel even asked William to become his business partner. He offered him a plot of land to build on near their house. Annie, how on earth could I compete with that? Not to mention the car and television!"

Annie's lips pulled upward into a grin. At the same time, though, she stiffened and absorbed what her friend had gone through. Rebecca's conflict with William definitely matched what she faced with Levi. Rebecca's may even have been worse. Several thoughtful moments of silence passed as they studied each other. Finally, Annie asked the obvious question. "Was there something you did that . . ."

Rebecca finished the question. "Made his decision for him? No. It was up to him. But when I considered the big picture, William leaving the faith wasn't even the worst of it."

"Really?"

Rebecca shook her head. "The biggest problem I faced was what to do if he actually left."

"My goodness."

Rebecca blinked. "It was a lose-lose situation." She shrugged her shoulders. "To stay Amish meant losing my true love. I couldn't imagine being without William. On the other hand, to have a life with him meant giving up my faith."

Annie's pulse danced to an uncertain tempo as she shook her head in disbelief. "Which did you pick?"

Rebecca hesitated. A rebellious hair slid down her cheek, and she shoved the honey-brown strand back under her *kapp*. "I struggled with that heavy question most of my time at the Conrads. Every night I read scripture, hoping for a crystal-clear answer. And finally . . ." Rebecca took a deep breath. "I got my answer. That it was in God's hands. Basically, that was what Old Sam had told me, too."

Annie's mind flitted from thought to thought. She'd had no idea Rebecca's marriage to her childhood sweetheart had endured such a storm.

"Now that it's over, it's easier to see what really was

going on. When you think about it, Annie, God's plan for everyone is already decided. So no matter how much I worried, in the end God would make the decision that would affect William and me for the rest of our lives. And it would be His will."

Intrigued, Annie didn't move. The only sound was the wind making the house creak.

"I decided my heart would always be Amish, no matter which way I went. That meant I would leave the faith for William."

Annie's heart nearly stopped. "Rebecca!"

Rebecca put her finger to her lips. "Shh! You're the only one who knows this. But I'm telling you because I believe it will make you realize you're not alone. You're certainly not the only Amish girl to be challenged." She moved in her chair and sighed. "Sometimes love carries a high price. In my case, the cost was my faith. But the more I thought about it, being Amish is much more than wearing my hair pulled back under a *kapp* and following the rules, though many would disagree. It's about more than my dress or not having air conditioning. In my heart, my faith would always be who I was."

She lowered her voice so it was barely audible. "Annie, I decided to stay with William."

The statement left Annie speechless. She swallowed. "Rebecca, I can't believe what you went through. I would never have dreamed it. You seem so . . . perfect."

Rebecca grinned. "Trust me, I'm not. Oftentimes things aren't what they appear on the surface. But God sent a miracle our way."

"What happened?"

"Fortunately, I wasn't the only one struggling with the situation. William was battling it, too. Maybe more. Apparently, wanting the luxuries of the English life was causing him huge guilt. And his mamma played a big role in what happened, I think." Rebecca hesitated. "You remember that it was her unspoken wish that he be raised Amish?"

Annie nodded.

"That's a tough thing to betray. And he loved his mamma. Just as I love mine. Not only that, but everything his aunt and uncle had taught him really stuck. He realized more than ever the huge sacrifice they'd made to raise him. His love and respect for them played a large role in his decision. Even though he was glad he'd had a major breakthrough with his relationship with his dad, at the same time he was obligated to reciprocate all his aunt and uncle had done for him. He couldn't let them down. They deserved so much from him."

Annie smiled. "They're good people."

Rebecca's eyes widened. "The best. So . . . whatever William did wasn't going to lead to a perfect ending. And when he eventually realized that, his decision became more evident. In the end, he chose what his heart told him to: the Amish faith."

"Thank God." Annie paused, putting her finger against her chin. "I'm happy for you both." She tried to conceal the slight skepticism she still felt. But curiosity got the best of her and she asked what was on her mind. "But what about the sports channel? The car?"

Rebecca threw her head back and laughed. She sat back in her chair, her eyes lit up with happiness. "Every tough decision involved a sacrifice. And to William, staying in the faith was worth what he gave up. I guess that despite the temptations, his roots were too strong. And I thank God every night that he decided as he did."

Annie blew out a deep breath. "What a story! I'm really glad you shared it, Rebecca. Your trust in me means a lot."

A thoughtful silence ensued before Rebecca posed a question to Annie. "So what about you and Levi? Has he considered joining the faith?"

Annie contemplated her question. Finally, she threw her hands in the air. "I don't know. The shunning left him with a bad taste. I'm not sure he could ever return to the faith that booted his family out of town."

Rebecca held up a hand to stop her. "Hold on, Annie. Let's go back to square one. His folks . . . they left of their own free will, right?"

Annie nodded. "But what choice was there?"

Rebecca pressed her lips together in deep concentration. She waved a hand in the air. "No one forced them to move. And from what I know, John Miller never asked for forgiveness. To me, it seems as if he was going to drive that truck no matter what." Rebecca held up her hand. "Forgive me for sharing my opinion, but as an outsider with little knowledge, that's how it looked."

Annie shrugged. "I suppose."

"Our rules are pretty well defined and he knew them."

"Maybe. But still . . . I'd like to give him the benefit of the doubt. Even if it was his fault, what happened was so cruel. No matter what you did, Rebecca, I don't know if I could ever see you on the street and not wave."

Rebecca nodded. "I know. The punishment does seem harsh. Thank goodness there aren't many shunnings. I can't rewrite the *Ordnung*. It is what it is. Maybe it's not perfect, but neither is life." She looked down at the bunch of flowers she'd been arranging as she spoke. "But, Annie, this isn't really about the shunning. Or John Miller. The most important question has to do with you and Levi."

She cleared her throat. "If I've learned anything about relationships, it's that they're nothing without communication. I've told what we went through. But from the get-go, I was straightforward with William. It's not easy opening your heart, but if I hadn't?" She closed her eyes and breathed in. "I wouldn't be with my true love. It works both ways. William was honest with me. I know confessing his longing to be English wasn't easy, but I'm so glad it came out when it did. The longer you hold in your thoughts, the more difficult it is to fix whatever problem is lingering. Annie, what about your lines of communication with John Miller's son? Where are you?"

While Annie considered an answer, Rebecca placed a dried rose into the arrangement. After a brief silence, Rebecca focused on Annie again. "Surely he knows how you feel about him?"

Annie swallowed the knot in her throat and nodded. "He mentioned getting married, but he won't be Amish. We can't be together because of what happened with his dad. It's our differences in faith."

"Annie, you're giving up your dream before you even give it a chance. Are you sure you can't be together?"

Was she positive? Rebecca had a point; Annie hadn't actually discussed the subject with Levi in depth. But did she need to? She had merely assumed being with him was impossible. Was it true that she was giving up a relationship before trying to make it work?

Finally, her answer came. "Rebecca, it can't work. My heart tells me so."

Rebecca gave an uncertain roll of her eyes. "Annie, does Levi love you?"

For some reason, the question caught Annie off guard; she wasn't sure how to respond. Her breath caught in her throat as she decided on a straightforward answer. But did she know the answer?

"Jah." Annie's heart suddenly pumped to a more hopeful beat. But she didn't want to believe in something she wanted more than anything in the world and not have it.

"I don't know what to do, Rebecca. Since he left, I've felt like part of me is missing. I knew losing him would be hard, but I had prepared myself for that. But what I didn't expect was how devastated I would be. It's hard to wake up in the morning knowing I'm without him. Not even Mamma's cream of celery soup tastes right anymore."

Rebecca tapped her fingers against the table. Her expression was unreadable.

"In my heart, I know there's no use pursuing a man who isn't of the faith. I'm sure you won't disagree."

Rebecca pressed her lips together.

"It's just so hard because we grew up together. If I'd never known him, things would be different. I wish his father hadn't been shunned."

"But that doesn't change reality. Most of what we face in life is out of our control, unfortunately. That's why faith is so important. Without it, how would we make it through life? I believe our strength and self-respect are determined by how we deal with such situations."

Annie raised a thoughtful brow.

"God doesn't always make things easy, Annie. Nobody knows that better than me."

Annie lowered her chin and nodded.

"But just look at William and me. It goes to show that there *are* happy endings. And a big part of that is making them happen. I hope you'll think about my story and realize anything's possible with God. But sometimes we have to figure out what He wants us to do. Prayer is the answer, Annie. That's how I finally came to peace with my situation with William."

Annie glanced at the dried arrangement Rebecca had put together during their conversation. With a gentle finger, she touched one of the deep blue buds and took in the beauty of every stem and flower.

She looked up and locked gazes with the creative woman. "That's absolutely gorgeous!"

Rebecca beamed. "Thank you! It's too bad we Amish aren't more in to this type of thing, but at least I get to make these wonderful bouquets and sell them to folks who will enjoy them as much as I do."

Annie stood, and Rebecca did the same. As they walked to the entryway of the house, Annie wrapped her arms around her new best friend. "Rebecca, thank you for talking with me and sharing your story. It gives me hope that God will somehow let me spend my life with Levi."

"The first thing you need to do—besides pray of course—is to figure out whether you truly want to spend the rest of your life with him. For sure. If you decide you do, the next step is to tell him how you feel. Bare your soul to him." Rebecca gave a casual roll of her shoulders. "Otherwise your dream can't come true."

Annie smiled a little.

As if suddenly realizing something, Rebecca raised her chin and placed her finger under Annie's chin in a sisterly way. "Think of all the different pieces in the arrangement I just made. Each unique stem and flower could be compared to your feelings for Levi."

Annie frowned. "I don't understand."

"Look at it this way: Everything you and Levi have gone through, including when he left town the first time and the last . . . plus all the times you've spent together . . . in a way, they're just like my arrangement. Right now, it's probably difficult for you to imagine that all those parts of your life with Levi might eventually come together to create a perfect ending, like the flowers in this beautiful piece. But for it to look the way it does, I had to position each individual plant the right way. If I hadn't actually taken these flowers and worked them, the piece wouldn't have happened. You've got to play a role in your future, Annie. If you want something, make it happen."

Annie gave a slow nod. "I get it."

"With God, anything's possible. We might not see it because we're human. But He has something in store for each and every one of us. And there's no way to even guess what the end result of His plan is. Before we get to our final destination, there will be ups and downs."

"Of course," Annie said with a smile. "Life isn't perfect."

"Exactly. Along the path God created for us, there will be bumps in the road. We've got to learn to get over them without being hurt. And in the end, I believe He has nothing but blessings awaiting us."

"I hope God will let me be with Levi forever."

"Pray about it, Annie. And I'll keep you and Levi in my prayers. I can see you truly love him. Just think of my story about almost losing William. It was a rocky road, and we nearly didn't make it to the too-good-to-be-true ending. But God worked His magic. And I'm sure He has a plan for you to be with Levi."

"But you're forgetting . . . Levi's English." As Annie considered what was against her, reality hit her like a splash of cold water in the face. She should never have opened up about her feelings for Levi. For several blissful moments, listening to Rebecca, Annie had actually believed her dream of marrying Levi might come true.

When she returned her attention to Rebecca, Annie took in the amused expression on her face. She clasped Annie's hands in hers. Immediately, reassuring warmth traveled up Annie's arms and landed in her shoulders. It was as if Rebecca had transferred her assurance to Annie. "Thank you, Rebecca," she said. "You've given me a lot to think about."

Chapter Twelve

From inside the open three-car garage, Levi waved to the mailman as he drove away. The friendly gesture was returned before the carrier slipped around the corner. Above, the sun shone its brightest. Levi squinted and stepped into the light.

The cold November temperature made the hairs on his forearms stand upright. His cotton long-sleeved shirt was rolled up past the wrists; he had been sketching his dream house on the kitchen table.

He stepped back into the house, breathing in delight at the warm contrast to outside. As he dropped the letters on the table, they separated. He glimpsed his name on one envelope and immediately pulled it from the scattered pile. His heart nearly stopped when he saw Annie's name and address on the upper left-hand corner.

Quick steps took him to his room. With one motion, he closed his door and sat down at his desk in front of the window overlooking the large backyard. Without wasting time, he pulled out the note, his heart picking up to the speed of a runner at the finish line of a race.

Dear Levi,

I hope you're well. As I write this, I'm remembering our last day together at Pebble Creek. Since then, I've not been able to forget you and our love for each other. I ache when I think of the man I gave up for my faith. My heart broke when I said good-bye. It will never be repaired. But even so, I can surely share this sentiment with you. I feel that this will be a sort of a cleansing.

Levi tried to swallow the knot in his throat, touching the note to his chest as he closed his eyes and drew a deep, anxious breath. Commanding his pulse to slow, he opened his eyes and continued reading.

I know I'm living up to my reputation as an Amish girl, but I share this with you because I'm opening my soul to you as never before. By giving you this journal page, you will have a part of me to keep with you forever.

He reread that last line before continuing.

It was difficult deciding whether to send this entry. At first I planned to keep it in my hope chest. After much thought, I realized how deeply I love you, and that if I didn't tell you how I felt the day we said good-bye, you would never know. And I want you to. Levi, I might never experience true love again. It seems a shame not to share something so rare and precious with the very person who is the root of this strong feeling. I would have told you more at Pebble Creek, but when you said you loved me, I was so happy yet so devastated that we couldn't be together, I was at a loss for words. Know that while you read this and my journal, I am thinking of you and keeping a special place for your love in my heart. By giving you this reflection of my love, I offer you a piece of my soul. Forever, Annie

As Levi put what he'd already read beneath the second page, a tear slipped down his cheek. His jaw dropped in surprise as he reread what she'd written. Afterward, he sat on the edge of his bed and drew in a deep breath. As he bent to focus on the potent words, his tears wouldn't stop.

He thought of his recent conversation with his dad. He reread Annie's words until he knew them by heart. The imprint of the four-leaf clover was barely visible, as if it were a ghost. But the message was real. Like Annie's feelings for him. And his for her.

In late November, Levi's mind continued to be focused on Annie's letter. And the fire. And everything else that had followed. He eyed the stones to be set above the fireplace. After the job was finished, a newly married couple would move in.

A voice interrupted his thoughts. "Son . . ."

Levi glanced at his dad. For long moments, their eyes locked. Levi wasn't sure if it was his imagination, but since he'd come home, his folks had seemed more emotional than usual. His mother had asked for his request for supper every day. His dad had even told him he loved him.

"Yeah, Dad?"

His father stepped forward to pat him on the shoulder. "I want you to know I've been thinking a lot lately." He paused to sniff and run the back of his hand over his nose. Levi was quick to detect the shiny moisture in his eyes. "I'm proud of you, son." He nodded his head. "I want you to know that." He gave a sudden shake of his head. "I can't get what happened out of my mind. What you did to save little Jake . . . well, there's only one word for it: brave."

Levi grinned and lowered his head in embarrassment. "Come on, Dad. You give me too much credit. If you'd been in my place, you would have done the same thing."

"I would hope so, but I'm not sure. Jake is one lucky boy." He chuckled. "What's he like?"

Levi thought for a moment. He realized his dad had never met his youngest nephew. After Levi's accident, Jake had come to the hospital once, but not at the same time Levi's parents were there. In fact, this was the first time his dad had brought up anyone in the family since their move. He gave a nudge to his dad's arm. "Let's sit down. It's break time anyway."

Side by side, they sat on the truck's tailgate on the unusually warm fall day. As Levi opened his thermos, he said, "You asked about Jake . . ."

His dad took a swig of water. "Does he look like his father?"

Levi grinned. "Kind of. He actually resembles me."

His dad slapped a friendly hand on Levi's thigh and moved closer to him. "No kidding?"

Levi nodded. "And he follows me around like I'm his big brother. He's pretty smart for his age, I think." He paused for a moment to press his palms against his cheeks. A strange sensation swept through him.

"You okay?"

He barely heard his father's question. The particular moment during the fire that he had struggled to recall—the frustrating void in his memory—appeared vividly in his mind as if the incident had happened just the day before. As he envisioned Jake in the path of the flying barn panel, Levi remembered throwing himself in front of the little boy. A shiver swept up his body. He shuddered. Then he smiled with great relief. "Dad, I just remembered rescuing Jake."

His dad's jaw dropped in surprise before giving him a huge pat on the back. "Good, son. Glad to hear it. Your mother and I have worried about your not getting full recall."

It took several moments for Levi to find his voice. Finally, he took a deep sigh. "A lot of people watched the barn burn. I was busy trying to put out the flames. There was an explosion. That's when everyone ran away. I wasn't far from Jake when a huge piece flew off the building. It was going to hit my cousin. My reaction was automatic. I threw myself in front of him."

Levi tried to calm the unusually fast rising and falling of his chest. He felt whole again. He'd finally remembered what had landed him in the hospital.

Whew. "Dad, I wish you and the family could be close again. Like old times."

He wasn't sure he'd ever dare to say the words; now, he figured it was as good a time as any.

Before he could continue, his dad was shaking his head. "Son, don't even go there. What's done is done. The *Ordnung* will never change. Neither will my family." He threw his hands in the air. "I mean, they can't. Even if they wanted me to be part of their lives, the church would never allow the kind of closeness you're asking for. The rules are strict."

Levi's sudden happiness evaporated like steam from a teakettle. He had dared to dream. He'd wanted to end the division between them. Not because of his relatives but because of Annie. For a moment, he'd imagined a world where he and the woman he loved could be on the same team.

But to Levi's surprise, his dad added, "What happened was a wake-up call to me. I'd like to be close to my brother and his family. I wish it could happen."

An unexpected sense of hope and excitement welled up in Levi's chest until he thought it might burst. And in the back of his mind were his uncle's words, spoken at his bedside: *We are indebted to you. If you ever need anything . . .*

He'd surely meant what he'd said. As Levi eyed the window, a squirrel caught his attention. Levi swallowed the lump that had formed in his throat. With full clarity, he remembered following little Jake outside to feed the animals.

Jake's pet. Friend. The recollection was so vivid, it seemed real.

He wondered why, all of a sudden, he yearned for family unity. *Because I've reconnected with them and I miss them, especially little Jake. And because I want to be with Annie.*

Levi waited for Annie at Pebble Creek. He wrung his hands together as an unusually cold November wind caressed the top of the water, making it appear frost white. Automatically, he pulled the sides of his hat down over his ears.

But the cold couldn't stop him from meeting her. He had something to tell her. *At their spot. It couldn't wait.*

"Levi!"

He responded with a big wave. When he checked his watch, a huge grin pulled the corners of his lips up. She was actually on time.

She wore a coat over her long dress and smiled as quick steps brought her toward him. He met her halfway.

"Annie!"

A laugh that was a combination of nervousness and intense excitement escaped her. "I was so happy when you called. I'm glad you're back. Even if it's for a short time," she added.

He took her cold hand in his. "I'm here on business."

As they neared the creek, he smiled at the surprised expression in her eyes.

"Are you and your dad building a new house in the area?"

Finally, they reached their creek-side path. He

ignored her question and hugged her. To his dismay, he sounded out of breath. "I'm so glad to see you. I've missed you."

The pitch of her voice softened. "I've missed you, too." She paused. "Whatever you've got to tell me must be important."

He nodded. "You feel like a walk up the hill?"

"Uh-huh."

In silence, they proceeded to their two flat stones and sat side by side.

In front of them, Pebble Creek gurgled as ice-cold water cascaded over rocks.

He faced her and swallowed. His hands shook. Why was he so nervous? He was at his special spot. With his favorite person.

She looked into his eyes. "I'm so happy you're back! How long will you be here?"

He ignored the question and said, "Annie, I have a lot to tell you." He pushed out a nervous laugh. "I'm not sure where to start."

She clasped his hands in hers. "Why not at the beginning? Mamma gave me the day off." She giggled. "I have all sorts of time."

He cleared his throat. "I think the fire at my uncle's barn was a blessing in disguise."

Her eyes were confused.

"It sounds strange, I know, but it's true. It was a close call. But the recovery time really made me give serious thought to my life and what's most important to me. Things became clear. And I want to share them with you."

She waited for him to continue.

"Annie, being with little Jake, my family, and old

friends made me realize how important this place is to me. When I went home, I struggled to figure out where I belonged. I talked to my folks. But what really helped me to decide was your letter. And the page from your journal." He paused. "I know the words by heart. When I read it, everything became easy to understand."

He noticed she'd become very quiet.

"You said the most important thing in your life was your faith and that you would give it up to be with me. That Rebecca Conrad said God would always be with you, no matter what church you were in, and that your true love knew Christ as well, but *together forever* would never happen without one of us giving up something. That you would make the ultimate sacrifice to be with the man you want to be your partner and the father of your children."

She didn't respond. Long moments passed as she looked him in the eye. The dancing flecks there suddenly became still. But they reflected honesty and everything that was almost too good to be true.

"Levi, every moment I spent with you became more precious. I prayed and prayed to forget you so I could become a good Amish wife and mother." She drew in a deep breath and moved her hands to her lap. "But the moment I realized I would never have you as my partner was devastating. Because the end of my journey to find love had come. I'd found it but couldn't have it. When I finally realized we would never be together, I yearned to share my feelings with you so you could keep a part of me in your heart."

"I'm glad you wrote that letter."

"Maybe it was crazy." She shrugged. "Perhaps my dream of being with you forever was my imagination at work."

"I wanted to reply to your letter. But given the circumstances, I was careful not to get you in trouble. I knew that anything I wrote might be read by someone else. And that your community might not be so understanding of how you felt. So I came in person to tell you."

She started to stand, but with a gentle hand, he stopped her. He faced her, sitting close to her, so he could read her reaction of what he was about to say. He could smell cinnamon on her breath.

"Annie, I've learned things I wasn't aware of when I came to the wedding. I want to spend the rest of my life with you." He paused. "And I want little Jake and the rest of my family back."

He pressed his lips together thoughtfully. "Nothing's ever going to be perfect, even if I stay English."

Her eyes widened with a newfound excitement.

"If it's okay with you, I want us to join the Amish church and get married."

"Oh, Levi!" She put her hand over her mouth as if digesting what he'd just told her. Several moments later, the corners of her lips lifted into the biggest smile he'd ever seen. "God has answered all my prayers. I'm so happy . . ." Before she could continue, tears began to slip down her cheeks. "How will it work? I mean, I want our families to be close, too."

Automatically, they started to walk. "Like I said, things can't be perfect, but my uncle committed to something while I was in the hospital. He was indebted to me for saving little Jake and said he would do anything for me."

Annie's jaw dropped.

"I've asked him and my aunt to meet with my folks and at least consider making a way to stay closer."

"What did they say?"

"That they would."

She gave a happy sigh.

"I believe the fire was the answer to my prayers, Annie. I asked God to tell me my purpose. I'm sure He brought me here to save little Jake, but I'm also praying He'll bring my family closer." He held up a hand to stop whatever she was about to say. "You're always reminding me that God works miracles."

She looked up to the sky. So did he.

When their gazes finally locked, Levi was sure of his purpose. It was to be with Annie. The contents of her letter had turned out to be the recipe for true love. And those very words would be forever etched in his heart as Annie's recipe.

RECIPE

Delicious Sponge Cakes

1 cup cake flour
6 medium eggs, separated
1 cup sugar
1 tsp. vanilla
½ tsp. lemon extract
¼ cup cold water
1 tsp. cream of tartar
Frosting (optional)

Set oven to 325 degrees ten minutes before baking. Use a 10-inch tube pan—do not grease. Sift flour, measure, resift 3 times. Put egg whites into a mixing bowl. Put yolks into a separate bowl; gradually beat in half of the sugar (½ cup) with a rotary beater until so thick beater is difficult to turn, at least 5 minutes. With a wooden spoon, beat in flavorings. Now add flour and water alternately in 3 or 4 portions, beating vigorously after each. Now sift cream of tartar over whites and beat with clean rotary beater until stiff enough to form soft, shiny peaks, then add rest of sugar gradually and beat until shiny meringue forms pointed peaks that curve at tips. Use a rubber scraper to quickly fold yolk mixture into the whites lightly but thoroughly. Now flow batter into pan. Bake cake on bottom rack 1 hour or until it springs back when touched lightly with finger. Remove from oven; invert at once over large funnel or bottle if pan does not stand on tube or side supports. When cool, remove from pan like Angel Food. Frosting is optional. (You can also bake it in a circular ungreased cake pan.) Enjoy!

DON'T MISS

Rebecca's Bouquet

The last thing Rebecca Sommer dreamed her plan to marry would bring is a heart-wrenching choice. She thought she and her betrothed, William, would spend the rest of their lives in Illinois's heartland, raising a family in their close-knit Amish hometown. But when he must travel far out of state to save his ailing father's business, Rebecca braves her relatives' disapproval—and her own fears—to work by his side. And though she finds herself ever more in love with the dedicated, resourceful man he proves to be, William's growing interest in English ways may be the one challenge even her steadfast faith can't meet . . .

Available wherever books are sold.

Turn the page for an excerpt from *Rebecca's Bouquet* . . .

His announcement took her by surprise. Rebecca Sommer met William's serious gaze and swallowed. The shadow from his hat made his expression impossible to read.

"You're really leaving?"

He fingered the black felt on the brim. "I know what a shock this is. Believe me, I never expected to hear that Dad had a heart attack."

"Do they expect a full recovery?"

William nodded. "But the docs say it will be a while before he works again. Right now, they can't even guess at a time line. In the meantime, Beth's struggling to take care of him."

While Rebecca considered the news, the warm June breeze rustled the large, ear-shaped leaves on the catalpa tree. The sun peeked from behind a large marshmallow cloud, as if deciding whether or not to appear. In the distance, a sleek black gelding clomped its hooves against the earth.

Pools of dust stirred, swirling and quickly disappearing. Lambs frolicked across the parcel of pasture separating the Sommer home from Old Sam Beachy's bright red barn. From where they stood, Rebecca could barely glimpse the orange YIELD sign on the back of the empty buggy parked next to the house.

"I'm the only person Dad trusts with his business." William paused and lowered his voice. "Beth wants me to come to Indiana and run his cabinet shop, Rebecca."

The news caused a wave of anxiety to roll through Rebecca's chest. She wrung her hands together in a nervous gesture. A long silence ensued as she thought of William leaving, and her shoulders grew tense. Not even the light, sweet fragrance floating from her mother's rose garden could take away Rebecca's anxiety.

When she finally started to respond, William held up a defensive hand. "It's just until he's back on his feet. This may not be such a bad thing. The experience might actually benefit us."

Rebecca raised a curious brow. The breeze blew a chestnut-brown hair out of place, and she quickly tucked it back under her *kapp*. Her gaze drifted from his face to his rolled-up sleeves.

Tiny freckles decorated his nose, giving him a youthful appearance. But there was nothing boyish about his square jaw or broad shoulders that tried to push their way out of his shirt. Her heart skipped a beat. She lifted her chin, and their eyes locked in understanding.

William smiled a little. "One of these days, we'll run our own company." He winked. "Don't worry."

She swallowed the lump in her throat. For one blissful, hopeful moment, she trusted everything would be okay. It wasn't those simple two words that reassured her, but the tender, persuasive way William said them. The low, steady tone in which he spoke could convince Rebecca of almost anything.

The warm pink glow on his cheeks made Rebecca's pulse pick up speed. As he looked at her for a reaction, her lips lifted into a wide smile. At the same time, it was impossible to stop the nervous rising and falling of her chest.

She'd never dreamed of being without William. Even temporarily. At the young age of eighteen, she hadn't confronted such a difficult issue.

But her church teachers and parents had raised her to deal with obstacles. Fortunately, they had prepared her to be strong and to pray for guidance. As she stared at her beloved flower garden, her thoughts became more chaotic.

The clothes on the line rose and fell with the warm summer breeze. Their fresh, soapy scent floated through the air. She surely had greater control over her destiny than the wet garments, whose fate was dependent on the wind. She and William could get through this. They loved each other. God would take care of them, wouldn't He?

She glanced up at William. The way the sun hit him at an angle made him look even taller than his six feet and two inches. He'd always been bigger and stronger than other kids his age.

The gray flecks in his deep blue eyes danced to a mysterious tune as he darted her a grin. When she looked into those dark pools, she could drown in happiness. But today, even the warmth emanating from his smile couldn't stop the concern that edged her voice. "Don't worry? But I do, William. What about . . ."

"Us?"

She nodded.

He leveled his gaze so that she looked directly at him. "Nothing has changed. We'll still get married in November after the harvest."

Rebecca hesitated. She couldn't believe William would really leave Arthur, Illinois. But his reason was legitimate. His father needed him. She wasn't selfish, and asking him to stay would be.

Circumstances were beyond her control. What could she do? The question nagged at her until frustration set in. Within a matter of minutes, her world had changed, and she fought to adjust. She nervously tapped the toe of her black shoe against the ground.

As she crossed her arms over her chest, she wished they could protect her from the dilemma she faced. Her brows narrowed into a frown, and a long silence ensued. She looked at him, hoping for an answer. Seeking even a hint of a solution.

To her surprise, William teased, "Rebecca, stop studying me like I'm a map of the world."

His statement broke the tension, and she burst into laughter because a map of the world was such a far stretch from what she'd been thinking.

"Of course, you've got to help your folks, William. I know how much Daniel's business means to him. You certainly can't let him lose it. I can imagine the number of cabinets on order."

Surprised and relieved that her voice sounded steady, Rebecca's shoulders trembled as the thought of William leaving sank in. They'd grown up together and hadn't spent a day without seeing one another.

She stopped a moment and considered Daniel and Beth Conrad. Nearly a decade ago, William's mamma had died, and Daniel had married Beth.

He was a skilled cabinetmaker. It was no surprise that people from all over the United States ordered his custom-made pieces. Rebecca had seen samples of his elegant, beautiful woodworking.

A thought popped into Rebecca's mind, and she frowned. "William, you seem to be forgetting something very important. Daniel and Beth . . . They're English."

He nodded. "Don't think I haven't given that consideration."

"I don't want to sound pessimistic, but how will you stay Amish in their world?"

He shrugged. "They're the same as us, really."

She rolled her eyes. "Of course they are. But the difference between our lifestyle and theirs is night and day. How can you expect to move in with them and be compatible?"

William hooked his fingers over his trouser pockets, looked down at the ground and furrowed a brow. Rebecca smiled. She knew him so well. Whenever something bothered him, he did this. Rebecca loved the intense look on his face when he worried. The small indentation in his chin intensified.

What fascinated her most, though, were the mysterious gray flecks that danced in his eyes. When he lifted his chin, those flecks took on a metallic appearance. Mesmerized, Rebecca couldn't stop looking at them.

Moments later, as if having made an important decision, he stood still, moved his hands to his hips, and met her gaze with a nod.

In a more confident tone, he spoke. "It will be okay, Rebecca. Don't forget that Dad was Amish before he married Beth. He was raised with the same principles as us. Just because he's English now doesn't mean he's forgotten everything he learned. No need to worry. He won't want me to change."

"No?"

William gave a firm shake of his head. "Of course not. In fact, I'm sure he'll insist that I stick to how I was brought up. Remember, he left me with *Aenti* Sarah and Uncle John when he remarried. Dad told me that raising me Amish was what my mother would have expected. The *Ordnung* was important to her. And keeping the faith must have also been at the top of Dad's list to have left me here. Nothing will change, Rebecca."

Rebecca realized that she was making too much out of William's going away. After all, it was only Indiana. Not the North Pole! Suddenly embarrassed at her lack of strength, she looked down at the hem of her dress before gazing straight into his eyes. He moved so close, his warm breath caressed her bottom lip, and it quivered. Time seemed to stand still while she savored the silent mutual understanding between them. That unique, unexplainable connection that she and William had.

"I've always read that things happen for a reason," William mentioned.

"Me too." Rebecca also knew the importance of the *Ordnung*. And she knew William's mamma,

Miriam, would have wanted him to stay in the faith that had meant everything to her.

As if sensing her distress, he interlaced his fingers together in front of him. His hands were large. She'd watched those very hands lift heavy bales of hay.

"Who knows? Maybe this is God's way of testing me."

Rebecca gave an uncertain roll of her eyes. "Talk to your aunt and uncle. They'll know what's best. After all, they've raised you since your father remarried."

The frustration in William's voice lifted a notch. "I already did. It's hard to convince them that what I'm doing is right." He lowered his voice. "You know how they feel. When Dad left the faith, he deserted me. But even so, I can't turn my back on him."

"Of course not."

"*Aenti* Sarah's concerned that people will treat me differently when I come back. She wants to talk to the bishop and get his permission. If that makes her feel better, then I'm all for it."

"If he'll give his blessing."

William nodded in agreement.

"But we're old enough to think for ourselves, William. When we get married and raise our family, we can't let everyone make up our minds for us."

He raised a brow. "You're so independent, Miss Rebecca."

She smiled a little.

A mischievous twinkle lightened his eyes.

"Your decision shouldn't be based on what people think," Rebecca said. "If we made choices to please others, we'd never win. Deep down inside, we have to be happy with ourselves. So you've got to do what's in your heart. And no one can decide that but you."

The expression that crossed his face suddenly became unreadable. She tilted her head and studied him with immense curiosity. "What are you thinking?"

His gray flecks repeated that metallic appearance. "Rebecca, you're something else."

A surge of warmth rushed through her.

"I can't believe your insight." He blinked in amazement. "You're an angel." His voice was low and soft. She thought he was going to kiss her. But he didn't. William followed the church rules. But Rebecca wouldn't have minded breaking that one.

In a breathless voice, she responded, "Thank you for that."

As if suddenly remembering the crux of their conversation, William returned to the original topic. "I've assured *Aenti* Sarah and Uncle John that I won't leave the Amish community. That I'll come back, and we'll get married. They finally justified letting me leave by looking at this as an opportunity to explore *Rumspringa*."

Rebecca grinned. "I guess that's one way to look at it." *Rumspringa* was the transition time between adolescence and adulthood when an Amish youth could try things before deciding whether to join the faith for him—or herself. She even had a friend who had gone as far as to get a driver's license.

He paused. "Rebecca, I know we didn't plan on this." His voice grew more confident as he continued. "You've got to understand that I love you more than anything in the world. Please tell me you'll wait for me. I give you my word that this move is only temporary. As soon as Dad's on his feet again, I'll come home. Promise."

As William committed, Rebecca took in his dark brown hair. The sun's brightness lightened it to the color of sand. For a moment, his features were both rugged and endearing. Rebecca's heart melted.

Her voice softened. "How long do you think you'll stay?"

William pressed his lips together thoughtfully. "Good question. Hopefully, he'll be back to work in no time. His customers depend on him, and according to Beth, he has a long list of orders for cabinets to produce and deliver. He's a strong man, Rebecca. He'll be okay."

"I believe that. I'll never forget when he came into town last year to see you." She giggled. "Remember his fancy car?"

William chuckled. "He sure enjoys the luxuries of the English. I wish our community wouldn't be so harsh on him. He's really Amish at heart."

William hesitated. "I used to resent that he left me."

Long moments passed in silence. He stepped closer and lowered his voice to a whisper. "Rebecca, you've become unusually quiet. And you didn't answer my question."

She raised an inquisitive brow.

"Will you wait for me?"

Her thoughts were chaotic. For something to do, she looked down and flattened her hands against her long, brown dress. She realized how brave William was and recalled the scandal Daniel Conrad had made when he married outside of the faith and had moved to the country outside of Evansville, Indiana. She raised her chin to look at William's face. Mamma always told her that a person's eyes gave away his feelings.

The tongue could lie. But not the eyes. William's intriguing flecks had become a shade lighter, dancing with hope and sincerity. His cheeks were flushed.

"William, you've got to do this." She let out a small, thoughtful sigh. "I remember a particular church sermon from a long time ago. The message was that our success in life isn't determined by making easy choices. It's measured by how we deal with difficult issues. And leaving Arthur is definitely a tough decision."

He hugged his hands to his hips. "What are you getting at?"

She quietly sought an answer to his question. What did she mean? She'd sounded like she knew what she was talking about. Moments later, the answer came. She recognized it with complete clarity.

She squared her shoulders. "I promised you I'd stick by you forever, William. And right now, you need me."

He gazed down at her in confusion.

Clearing her throat, she looked up at him and drew a long breath. "I'm going with you."

Inside Old Sam Beachy's barn, Rebecca poured out her dilemma to her dear friend. Afterwards,

Buddy whimpered sympathetically at her feet. Rebecca reached down from her rocking chair opposite Old Sam's workbench and obediently stroked the Irish setter behind his ears. The canine closed his eyes in contentment.

Old Sam was famous for his hope chests. He certainly wasn't the only person to put together the pieces, but he was a brilliant artist who etched beautiful, personalized designs into the lids.

Rebecca had looked at his beloved Esther as a second mother. Since she'd succumbed to pneumonia a couple of years ago, Rebecca had tried to return her kindness to the old widower. So did her friends, Rachel and Annie. The trio took care of him. Rachel listened to Sam's horse-and-buggy stories. Annie baked him delicious sponge cakes while Rebecca picked him fresh flowers.

Drawing a long breath, Rebecca wondered what advice he'd give. Whatever it was would be good. Because no one was wiser than Old Sam. She crossed her legs at the ankles. Sawdust floated in the air. Rebecca breathed in the woodsy smell of oak.

When he started to speak, she sat up a little straighter. "The real secret to happiness is not what we give or receive; it's what we share. I would consider your help to William and his parents a gift from the heart. At the same time, a clear conscience is a soft pillow. You want to have the blessing of our bishop and your parents. The last thing you want is a scandal about you and William living under the same roof."

Rebecca let out a deep, thoughtful sigh as she

considered his wisdom. In the background, she could hear Ginger enter her stall from the pasture. Old Sam's horse snorted. And that meant she wanted an apple.

Sam's voice prompted Rebecca to meet his gaze. "Rebecca, I can give you plenty of advice. But the most important thing I can tell you is to pray."

Rebecca nodded and crossed her arms over her chest.

"But remember: Do not ask the Lord to guide your footsteps if you're not willing to move your feet."

Rebecca was fully aware that William was ready to leave. In her front yard, she hugged her baby sister, Emily, shoving a rebellious strand of blond hair out of her face. Rebecca planted an affectionate kiss on brother Peter's cheek. "Be good."

Pete's attention was on Rebecca just long enough to say good-bye. As she turned to her father, the two kids started screaming and chasing each other in a game of tag. Emily nearly tripped over a chicken in the process. Rebecca was quick to notice the uncertain expression on Old Sam's face.

The sweet, creamy smell of homemade butter competed with the aroma of freshly baked bread. Both enticing scents floated out of the open kitchen windows. Tonight, Rebecca would miss Mamma's dinner. It would be the first time Rebecca hadn't eaten with her family.

Her heart pumped to an uncertain beat. But

she'd never let her fear show. Ever since the death of her other little sister, Rebecca had learned to put on a brave façade. Her family depended on her for strength.

Rebecca's father grasped her hands and gave them a tight squeeze. She immediately noted that his arms shook. It stunned her to realize that his embrace was more of a nervous gesture than an offer of support. And the expression on his face was anything but encouraging. Rebecca understood his opposition to what she was about to do. Her father's approval was important to her, and it bothered her to seem disrespectful.

All of her life, she'd tried hard to please him. They'd never even argued. In fact, this was the first time she'd gone against his wishes. But William was her future. She wanted to be by his side whenever he needed her.

In a gruff, firm voice, her father spoke. "Be careful, Becca. You know how I feel. I'm disappointed that William hasn't convinced you to stay. You belong here. In Arthur."

He pushed out a frustrated breath. "But you're of age to make your own decision. We've made arrangements with Beth so that living under the same roof with William will be proper. We trust she'll be a responsible chaperone while you're with the Conrads. Just come home soon. We need your help with chores."

He pointed an authoritative finger. "And never let the English ways influence you. They will tempt you to be like them, Becca. Remember your faith."

Rebecca responded with a teary nod. When she finally faced Mamma, she forced a brave smile. But the tightness in her throat made it difficult to say good-bye.

Mamma's deep blue eyes clouded with moisture. With one swift motion, Rebecca hugged her. For long moments, she was all too aware of how much she would miss that security. The protection only a parent could offer.

Much too soon, Mamma released her and held her at arm's length. When Rebecca finally turned to Old Sam, he stepped forward and handed her a cardboard container with handles.

She met his gaze and lifted a curious brow. "This is for me?"

He nodded. "I hope you like it." He pointed. "Go ahead. Take it out."

Everyone was quiet while she removed the gift. As she lifted the hope chest, she caught her breath. There was a unanimous sound of awe from the group. "Old Sam . . ." She focused on the design etched into the lid. "It's absolutely beautiful! I will treasure it the rest of my life."

"You always bring me fresh flowers, so I thought you'd like the bouquet."

She glanced at William before turning her attention back to Sam. "I'm taking the miniature hope chest with me."

Sam's voice was low and edged with emotion. "I will pray for your safety. And remember that freedom is not to do as you please, but the liberty to do as you ought. And the person who sows seeds of kindness will have a perpetual harvest. That's you, Rebecca."

Rebecca blinked as salty tears filled her eyes. With great care, she returned the hope chest to its box on the bright green blades of grass.

Old Sam's voice cracked. "You come back soon. And if you want good advice, consult an old man."

A grin tugged at Rebecca's lips. Sam knew every proverb in the book. She'd miss hearing him recount them.

"Thank you again. I can't wait to start putting away special trinkets for the children I will have some day."

When she looked up at him, he merely nodded approval.

William's voice startled her from her thoughts. "Rebecca, it's time to head out. It's gonna be a long drive."

Her gaze remained locked with Mamma's. Mary Sommer's soft voice shook with emotion. "This is the first time you've left us. But you're strong."

Rebecca squeezed her eyes closed for several heartbeats.

As if to reassure herself, her mother went on. "We hope Daniel recovers quickly. William needs you. In the meantime, God will keep both of you in His hands. Don't forget that. Always pray. And remember what we've taught you. Everything you've learned in church."

"Jah."

"It's never been a secret that God gave you a special gift for accepting challenges. I'll never forget the time you jumped into that creek to save your brother. You pulled him to shore."

Rebecca grinned. "I remember."

"*Rumspringa* might be the most important time in your life. But be very careful. There will be temptations in the English world. In fact, the bishop is concerned that you will decide against joining the Amish church."

"I know who I am."

A tear rolled down Mamma's cheek while she slipped something small and soft between Rebecca's palms. Rebecca glanced down at the crocheted cover.

"I put together this scripture book to help you while you're away, Rebecca. When you have doubts or fears, read it. The good words will comfort and give you strength. You can even share them with Beth. She's going through a difficult time. Your *daed* and I will pray for you every day." She paused. "Lend Daniel your support. The bishop wants you to set three additional goals and accomplish them while you're gone. Give them careful consideration. They must be unselfish and important. Doing this will make your mission even more significant."

After a lengthy silence, William addressed the Sommers in a reassuring voice. "I'll take good care of her. You can be sure of that."

Rebecca's dad raised his chin and directed his attention to William. "We expect nothing less."

Long, tense moments passed while her father and William locked gazes. Several heartbeats later, Eli Sommer stepped forward. "I don't approve of my

Becca going so far away. I'm holding you responsible for her, William. If anything happens . . ."

William darted an unsure glance at Rebecca before responding. "I understand your concern. That's why I didn't encourage her to come."

Rebecca raised her chin and regarded both of them. "I've given this a lot of thought. I'll go. And I'll come back, safe and sound."

Rebecca listened with dread as her father continued making his case. She knew William wouldn't talk back. And she wasn't about to change her mind about going.

"*Daed*, it's my decision. Please don't worry."

Before he could argue, she threw her arms around him and gave him a tight, reassuring hug. After she stepped away, William motioned toward the black Cadillac. As Rebecca drew a deep breath, her knees trembled, and her heart pounded like a jackhammer. Finally, she forced her jellylike legs to move. She didn't turn around as William opened her door.

Before stepping inside, Rebecca put Mamma's scripture book inside the hope chest. William took the box from her and placed it in the middle of the backseat. Rebecca brought very little with her. Just one small suitcase that her father placed in the trunk.

With great hesitation, she waved good-bye. She forced a confident smile, but her entire body shook. She sat very still as Daniel's second cousin, Ethan, backed the car out of the drive. Gravel crunched under the tires. This wasn't Rebecca's first ride in an automobile. Car rides were not uncommon in the Amish community.

Trying to convince herself she was doing the right thing, she gently pushed the down arrow by her door handle, and the window opened. Rebecca turned in her seat and waved until the sad faces of her family, their plain-looking wooden-framed house built by her great-grandfather, and Old Sam, disappeared.

William turned to her. A worry crease crept across his forehead. The cleft in his chin became more pronounced. "Rebecca, your dad's right. I should have made you stay. The last thing I want to do is create tension between you two."

"It wasn't your choice. As far as my father's concerned . . ." She gave a frustrated shake of her head. "I don't like displeasing him either. On the other hand, it's not right for me to stay here and send you off to save Daniel's shop all by yourself." She shrugged.

In silence, she thought about what she'd just said. She nervously ran her hand over the smooth black leather seat.

"You can adjust the air vents," Ethan announced, turning briefly to make eye contact with her.

She was thankful she didn't have to travel to the Indiana countryside by horse and buggy. She rather enjoyed the soft, barely audible purring of the engine.

Next to her, she eyed the cardboard and pulled out the mini hope chest, setting the box on the floor. She smiled a little.

"Old Sam is something else." William's voice was barely more than a whisper.

"*Jah.* I can't wait to tell him about our trip." Rebecca giggled. "I'll miss listening to him grumble while he works in the barn. I enjoy watching him make those elaborate chests that he sells to the stores in town."

William gave a small nod. "He loves you three girls."

"Thank goodness that Annie and Rachel will be around to keep him company."

The three friends had loved Esther. Now they took care of Old Sam. He was like an uncle to them. But Rebecca was leaving the world she knew. Would she fit in with the English?

4277

Visit us online at
KensingtonBooks.com
to read more from your favorite authors, see books by series, view reading group guides, and more.

Join us on social media
for sneak peeks, chances to win books and prize packs, and to share your thoughts with other readers.

facebook.com/kensingtonpublishing
twitter.com/kensingtonbooks

Tell us what you think!

To share your thoughts, submit a review, or sign up for our eNewsletters, please visit:
KensingtonBooks.com/TellUs.